The debarkation of the space freighter from Earth was in full swing. Passengers pressed out onto the landing platforms carrying luggage.

"These immigrant freighters certainly crowd them in," one of the watching men said.

The big man replied: "That's why they call them freighters. They handle human cargoes."

All three watched as a pretty girl passed by, carrying a suitcase. She had redgold hair, a firm, lithe body.

The big man watched her speculatively. Then he nodded. "She'll do," he said. "Pick her up and bring her to my apartment."

And from that moment, Evana Travis was doomed. . . .

PLANETS FOR SALE

□

A.E. Van VOGT
and
E. MAYNE HULL

tempo books

GROSSET & DUNLAP
Publishers   New York

PLANETS
FOR SALE

Chapter 1

The four men in the idling plane sat quiet now, watching. The debarkation of the space freighter from Earth was in full swing. People were pressing out onto the landing platforms carrying luggage. One of the men in the airabout sneered:

"These immigrant freighters certainly crowd them in."

The big man said, "That's why they call them freighters. They handle human cargoes."

"Look, Mr. Delaney!" a third man said excitedly. "There's a girl, a dazzler if I ever saw one."

The big man was silent. His sleet-gray eyes were narrowed on the girl who had paused twenty feet away. She had red-gold hair, a thin but determined face and a firm, lithe body. She carried one small suitcase.

"She is pretty," he admitted cautiously. His gaze followed the girl as she turned and walked slowly toward the distant exit. He nodded. "She'll do. Pick her up and bring her to my apartment."

He climbed out of the plane, watched it glide off after the girl, then stepped into a private speedster that instantly hurtled off into the sky.

Evana Travis walked along the Pedestrian Way toward the exit unaware of the machineful of men following her. She was trembling from the excitement of the landing, but her mind was still on the trip that had now ended.

She hadn't expected so much bigness. The very name—Ridge Stars—had a cozy sound. The picture of the system in her mind was of an intimately related group of suns pouring

1

a blaze of light into the surrounding heavens. Figures never had had much meaning for her; and growing up in a world where people said, "Why, that's only a thousand light-years!" somehow that had made of space an area as limited, in a different way, as Earth. Immigration-appeal folders did nothing to discourage her opinion.

The first shock had come on the twelfth day out when the loud-speakers announced that the Ridge was now visible to the naked eye. It was, all two hundred light-years of it, spread across the heavens. There were one hundred and ninety-four suns in the group, seventy of them as large as, or larger, than Sol—at least so the announcer shouted. Evana saw only pin points of light in a darkness which was but faintly relieved by a sprinkling of more remote stars.

Slowly, she admitted to herself that there *was* a resemblance to a ridge, and then all thought of the physical aspect of the stars ended as the announcer said, "—a vote will shortly be taken as to which planet of which sun the passengers of this ship will be landed on. The majority will decide and all must abide by the decision. Good-by for now."

For a moment Evana stood, too shocked to move. Then she was fighting her way through the crowded corridors and decks. She reached the captain's cabin, and was making her protest even as the door was banging shut behind her.

"What kind of outrage is this?" she demanded. "I'm going to my sister on the third planet of the Doridora sun. That's where I bought my ticket for, and that's where I'm going, vote or no vote."

The young man who sat behind the big desk in one corner of the small room looked at her calmly. "Don't be such an innocent," he said.

Evana stared at him. "What do you mean?"

His grinning face mocked her. He had blue eyes and a space-tanned face, and he looked about thirty. He said, "You're in space now, sister, far from the rigid laws of Earth. Where you're going, atomic engineering is building an operator-controlled universe, fortunes are made and lost every day, people die violently every hour, and the word of the big monopolists is the final authority."

He stopped. He studied Evana sardonically. He said, "It's a game, beautiful. And you've been caught in it. All the improvements in working conditions on Earth during the past fifty years were designed to prevent wholesale immigration to the newer worlds of the galaxy. The governments of the Ridge Star planets and other star groups have had to develop cunning counter attractions, including cutting the price of the trip to less than cost. That explains why it's impossible to do anything but dump each shipload *en masse*. This cargo, for instance, is headed for Delfi II."

"But," Evana said, "there's going to be a ballot taken as to which planet we land on. The announcer said—"

The young man laughed. "Oh, sure!" The mirth faded from his face. "And it's going to be all fair and square, too—pictures of each planet, short educational talks, an elimination vote every time four planets have been discussed—straight merit will decide the issue. But Delfi II will be selected because it's Delfi's turn, and so we're showing that planet to advantage, while the unpleasant side of the other planets gets top billing this trip. Simple, eh?"

As Evana shook her head in numb amazement, he went on, "Delfi's a grand place. Its capital city, Suderea, has four million population, with ninety buildings of more than a hundred stories all built by operators, men whose names are synonyms for wealth and power; and the greatest of them all is a young Norwegian-Englishman named Artur Blord. He's a byword. You'll hear his name in every town and village. In less than ten years he's made an astronomical fortune by outsmarting the big shots themselves. They exploit men; he exploits *them*. Why—"

"But you don't understand," Evana said desperately. "My sister expects me."

His answer was a shrug. "Look, lady, the Ridge Star governments have offered a prize for the invention of an interstellar drive that won't infringe existing Earth patents, but until that prize is won the only way you'll ever get off

3

Delfi II would be to get in good with some private spaceship owner. There just isn't any public transport.

"And now," he stood up, "I'm afraid you'll have to stay here in my cabin until that ballot has been taken. It's my policy to be honest with those who complain, but it means restrictions for them. Don't get alarmed! I have no personal designs on you, even though you wouldn't have a single comeback if I did have. But a man like myself, with seventeen wives on as many planets, thirty-eight kids, and a soft heart, can't afford to get mixed up with any more women."

He went out. The door clicked behind him.

And now, seven days later, here she was on the unwanted world of Delfi II.

Evana paused uncertainly at the great gate of the landing field. As she stood there staring down at the city below and the blue of the sea beyond she felt doubt and dread at the thought of her situation. There was a sound behind her. Rough hands smashed across her mouth, and grabbed her arms. She was lifted from the ground and through a door into a wingless plane that instantly curled up into the air like smoke rising from a chimney.

She began to twist and squirm, fighting the masked men who held her. But they were big and heavy and their very weight resisted her efforts to claw free. She felt the bump of the plane landing. The men caught her up again and carried her swiftly down a flight of stairs. Then she was in a room, falling toward a couch.

Lying down made things easier. The agony of exhaustion faded. The salty taste in her mouth began to go away. Her vision came slowly back into focus. She saw that she was in a magnificently furnished room. And, standing a dozen feet away, staring at her, was a powerful-looking man wearing a mask.

"Ah," said the man, "coming back to life, are you? Fine."

Recognition of the kind of mask he wore throttled the scream in her throat. There was the exact bulge at the mouth that she had seen so often in the movies, the bulge that was the machine which disguised the wearer's voice. The sight of such a device abruptly made the affair unreal, and Evana laughed. She stopped the laughter as she recognized the hysteria in it, and found her voice.

"I want to know the meaning of this," she gulped. "I'm sure there must be some mistake."

The big man swung around on her. "There's been no mistake," he said coldly. "I picked you up because you're a pretty and intelligent-looking girl. You're going to make a thousand stellors for yourself, and you're going to make it whether you like it or not. Now stop looking like a scared fool."

Evana tried to speak, and couldn't. It took a long moment to realize why. Relief! Relief so tremendous that it hurt deep down like food badly swallowed. Whatever was here, it wasn't death.

The man was speaking again, saying, "What do you know about the Ridge Stars?"

She stared blankly. "Nothing."

"Good." He loomed above her, seemingly satisfied. He went on, "What was your occupation on Earth?"

"I was a mechanical-filing-system operator."

"Oh!" His tone held disappointment. "Well, it doesn't matter," he said finally. "The employment agency will put an educator on you and make you into a passable private secretary in one hour."

His words held no real meaning for Evana. She was thinking that this was what the stories she had heard back home had meant, the stories that said that on the far planets the frontiers extended right into the biggest of the cities. This crude kidnapping of her from an interstellar landing field couldn't be anything but frontier.

The man fumbled in his pocket and drew out a small white card. He said, "Here's the name of your hotel. As soon as you're registered, go to the Fair Play Employment Agency, and they'll take care of you. I've written the address on the back of the card."

Evana took the card blankly and stuffed it unread into her purse. With wide eyes she watched the man pick up a small package from among the bottles on the table. She took the package with limp fingers when he held it out to her. He said, "Put this in your purse, too. There's a note inside that explains everything you need to know. And remember, there's a thousand stellors in it for you, if everything goes smoothly."

It didn't seem possible. It didn't seem reasonable. The man couldn't be such a fool as to let her walk out of here now, out of this apartment, trusting her to do as he wanted after she had gone out into the obscuring labyrinth of a vast city.

"Two more things," the man said softly, "and then you can leave. First, have you ever heard of seven-day poison?" He leaned forward as he spoke the words, and there was an intensity in his manner that, more than his words, brought a chill. She gasped, "It's the poison that feeds on the blood; and on the seventh day undergoes a chemical change that—" She saw the syringe in his hand then, and with a thin scream leaped to her feet. The man yelled:

"Grab her!"

She had forgotten the other men. They held her as the needle stabbed into her left leg above the knee. Then the needle was withdrawn and the men let her go. She half-fell, half-sank to the floor, sobbing.

"The beauty of that poison," the man said, "is that it can be made like a lock pattern, in many thousands of slight variations, but the antidote must have as its base a dose of the original poison, which as you can see is in my possession. Now, don't get hysterical." His tone became brutal. "I'll make up the antidote and it'll be here when you've accomplished what I want."

"But I don't know where 'here' is!" Evana cried desperately. "Suppose something happens to you—"

"The second thing," said her tormentor curtly, "is another kind of precaution. It's just possible that several days may pass before you will find the opportunity to accomplish my purpose, and that in the meantime the man whose secretary you are to become may want you to be his mistress. Now it's quite obvious we can't have any prissy scruples on your part so—*Hold her!*"

The second needle stabbed painfully into her arm just above the elbow. Above her, the man said, "O.K., take her out, drop her off near the hotel!"

When the door had closed behind Evana, Delaney slowly took off his mask. He stood for a moment then, a dark, brooding figure. Gradually, his heavy face wreathed into a grim smile. He picked up an eldophone and said, "Get me the president of the J. H. Gorder Atomic Power Company of the planet Fasser IV. Tell him Delaney's calling."

"One moment sir," the operator said.

A minute passed, then a click sounded and a very clear, strong voice said, "Gorder speaking. What's on your mind, Delaney?"

"All the initial moves against Artur Blord are now taken," Delaney said. "Tell the others, they can start arriving tomorrow morning at the Skal's castle. And advise the Skal that we're coming. Good-by."

Chapter 2

Sitting in her hotel room, Evana read the letter that was in the package Delaney had given her:

By the time you read this, you will have opened the package I gave you, and noted that it contains: (1) a cigaret case with cigarets in it; (2) a necklace with a watchlike pendant; (3) a package of white pills; (4) a V-shaped copper device; (5) a syringe.

The cigarets are doped. If circumstances permit, you will try to give one of them to the man who will be your employer beginning tomorrow. The circumstances, however, must be that you and he are alone, and that he is not suspicious of you. The case ejects two cigarets at a time, the outer one is doped, the inner one is not, always.

The white pills constitute a second line of attack. They can be used to drug such things as water, coffee, liquor; also they crumble easily and can be sprinkled over meat sandwiches, giving the appearance of salt.

The pendant is a radio device. As soon as Artur Blord, your future employer, is unconscious, unloosen the screw at the bottom and press the tiny bulb in the center. This will advise my men that you have taken the first step toward the accomplishment of our joint purpose.

The V-shaped copper device is designed to short-circuit the alarm system which Mr. Blord has installed on the top floor of his headquarters, which is located at 686 Financial Avenue. In order to employ this device properly it is necessary to understand the arrangement of rooms in Mr. Blord's penthouse.

The penthouse is divided into four main sections: the office, two apartments and a roof garden. The office is made up of three rooms, an anteroom, secretary's room and Mr. Blord's private office. From Mr. Blord's office a door leads to his personal eight-room apartment.

From the secretary's office there is an entrance to the other apartment, a small, four-room affair. This is where you will live, and I might say that the intimate implications of the arrangement are not misleading. Any unwillingness you may feel on the subject will be overcome by the incentives we have provided for an early successful conclusion of your mission. The great danger from the poison should restrain you from injudicious action.

Both apartments have French doors which open onto the roof garden; and it is beside the French door of Mr. Blord's apartment that you will find an ornate metal instrument with a slit in it. Slide the V-shaped device into this slit, point first, until the two translucent ends of the V light up.

Now, press the bulb of the pendant again. My men will arrive within a few minutes. You must accompany them if you want your antidote and your reward. Afterward, I will transport you to any of the Ridge Star planets you desire. Obviously, for your own safety, you cannot remain on Delfi II.

Item No. 5 in this package, the syringe, contains Nonchalant, a dose of which, taken tomorrow morning, will steady your nerves, keep color in your cheeks, no matter how great your inner nervousness. I advise you to take it every morning until you have succeeded in your purpose.

As soon as you have read this letter, go to the Fair Play Employment Agency, whose address is on the card I gave you. I warn you most earnestly there is no time to waste. Tomorrow the seven-day poison will have only six days to go.

Slowly, Evana folded the letter and slipped it into the drawer of the little table beside her chair. For a long moment she sat very still, holding her mind tight. Then she stood up, caught up her bag and the white card the man had given her, and left the room.

When she reached the street, she saw the neon sign less than a block away:

FAIR PLAY EMPLOYMENT AGENCY

Still not daring to think, she walked swiftly along the sidewalk. She did not pause when she reached the big door with its heavy gold lettering. She pushed it open and stepped into the huge, desk-cluttered office of the employment agency, and presently she was filling out her application.

She slept poorly that first night. She did remember in the morning to inject a dose of Nonchalant into the upper part of her arm. But through all the actions and thoughts and memories that flooded her mind ran one dominant strain of terror: She had to do what the masked man demanded with utter singleness of purpose. There wasn't any alternative.

The morning streets were packed, long wide boulevards of rushing human masses. Overhead streamed a countless swarm of airabouts. Number 686 Financial Avenue was a shining metal shaft of a building. It was narrow at the top, but at the bottom it spread over nine square blocks. Great avenues plowed through its base. Plane shafts crisscrossed its upper stories; and at about the fortieth floor was a sign that shone in the sun:

ARTUR BLORD HOLDING CO., LIMITED

Far back in Evana's mind was the thought that surely *she* wouldn't be hired as secretary by a man who must have tens of thousands of employees craving promotion to such a high position. But the girl at the reception desk inside the first main entrance stared enviously at her agency card and said, "Go straight up to the one hundred and ninetieth floor. I'll phone up to Mr. Magrusson."

At the one hundred and ninetieth floor, a plump, middle-aged man was waiting at the elevator. "I'm Mr. Magrusson," he said, "General Manager of the Artur Blord Holding Company." He smiled at her, his pale blue eyes watering. "While we depend on the Fair Play Agency to send us a girl suited to Mr. Blord's requirements, I must verify two things: You did arrive yesterday on the freighter from Earth? And this is your first job, not only on Delfi, but on any planet other than Earth?"

So it was her recent Earth origin that gave her such a startling preference. Evana drew a deep breath. "I swear it!" she said.

Magrusson gave a satisfied nod. "Good. We'll check that thoroughly, of course. But now, I'll take you up to the penthouse floor. Your living quarters are there, as well as the offices. Mr. Blord is expected shortly. In the meantime, you may as well familiarize yourself with the arrangement of your new headquarters. Come this way."

Evana followed him down the corridor to another elevator that carried them up to the penthouse floor. They went past a door marked "PRIVATE," then Magrusson opened a second door. He stepped back for her to enter, and said, "Everything on this floor is in your charge as of this moment. You may examine anything you please that isn't locked, and call me for any information you may require. Good luck, Miss Travis. We hope you'll be happy working with us." He smiled and nodded and went off down the hall.

To Evana the aloneness brought no peace. The depressing continuity of her thoughts suffered neither the restraint of interruption nor the easement of hope. All normal reaction was over-shadowed by the menacing words Magrusson had spoken. "Mr. Blord is expected shortly." The strain of that had no relation to anything she had ever endured.

Exploration did provide a brief excitement. But even there her pre-knowledge of the room arrangements cancelled the full effect. For the description in the letter was exact. Seeing the actuality simply filled in details. Her office was a large denlike room with books, a filing system, a desk equipped with automatic Recorders. There were several mechanical contrivances scattered along the walls at which she barely glanced.

The private office beyond was a larger version of the secretary's room, but without the filing system. She did not go into the eight-room apartment of Artur Blord, simply glanced in long enough to see the green foliage of the roof garden through the living-room windows. She really should, she thought, make sure that there was an energy device to cut the alarm system as the letter had stated. But—*Mr. Blord is expected shortly.*

She withdrew to the secretary's office. Slowly, her courage returned, but she made no attempt at further exploration. She began an elaborate examination of the mechanical filing system. It yielded nothing but detailed information about the geography of hundreds of planets.

She found herself frowning over the vast, detailed information about metals, forests, gems, valuable soils and of estimates of value that seemed to have no relation to the money estimates that were also given. There was a field of chromium on the planet Tanchion IV, value No. 1, one hundred billion stellors; value No. 2, just plain slogging. Let somebody else do it all.

The two-value system extended everywhere. For a forest on Tragona VII, the first value was: "All treasure wood; priceless. The second valuation said: "Dennis Kray operator. Hard, brilliant. Keep in mind."

She grew hungry, finally, and in surprise saw that it was two o'clock. At the same moment, she became aware of a reluctance to enter the apartment—her apartment now. She felt a rising anger against herself. She was being plain silly because she couldn't afford to indulge in, what was it the man had called it?—prissy scruples—now.

It was a woman's living room that greeted her eyes, and a woman's bedroom. Pastel colors made a splendid but muted pattern. Everywhere were frills, knickknacks, fluffy comforts, extras from store departments that men would never think of visiting. The femininity would be a constant reminder of its previous occupant—the last secretary-mistress who had now gone into some unexplained discard.

After she had satisfied her hunger, Evana sat frowning at the place. The frills would certainly have to go from the living room, she thought critically. A living room should be trim and comfortable, not littered with gew-gaws. One's femininity should show in the bedroom. She'd always dreamed of having a really costly canopied four-poster, and— She caught her mind in its gyrations, and sat appalled. She thought: This is really incredible. How can I ever think of accepting all this?

She stood up, and it was then for the first time that she saw the photograph. It was standing on the mantelpiece; and she knew instantly that she was looking at the picture of Artur Blord. It was the sensitive countenance of a man in his early thirties. The face was lean, with thin aristocratic nose, strong chin and firm, well-molded lips.

His appearance disturbed her; not that it could make any difference. She had to carry out her purpose. Momentarily, the recollection of that purpose made her head swim. She sank down on a sofa, and covered her face with her hands. When the dizziness passed, she looked once more at the photograph, and her mind went back to what the captain of the space freighter had said about the big financial and industrial operators in this part of the galaxy. Strange to think the man had even mentioned Artur Blord as the greatest of them all because—what was it the commander had said?—the others exploited men, and Blord exploited *them.*

She wondered vaguely in what way he had exploited the men who were obviously using her as their instrument of revenge. Or perhaps they had kidnapped her as part of a scheme to prevent such a situation occurring. Looking now at the picture of Blord, she tried to compare it with her memory of the men who had given her the seven-day poison— the men who literally held her life in their hands.

She must have dozed then, for she awakened with a start, and saw that it was dark. She felt a brief panic, but that ended as, through the huge window, she saw a great moon come out from behind a dark cloud. It gleamed through the window, filling the room with pale light. She went to the window and stared up at it, a globe of brightness ten times as big as Earth's satellite. The educational talks on the space freighter, she recalled, had proved it wasn't a moon at all, but a dead companion planet as large as Delfi II; and once, long before man came, there had been life on it. Evana's thoughts returned to her own situation. Funny how she had awakened with such a start as if—

Bzzz! The sound made her jump. And then she stood stiffly as a strong, clear, masculine voice said from a wall speaker:

"Miss Travis, Artur Blord speaking. Will you come to my office immediately, please."

13

Chapter 3

"I," Artur Blord was saying an hour later, "like new cities, new planets. They're soulless. They have no culture, no institutions with hardening of the arteries, nobody going around yelling for prohibition of this, that and the other. If a man's got a religion—and who hasn't?—he's not scheming to force it on others. Just a minute, here's something! Grab your recorder! It's for your private information."

Evana grabbed. For an hour she had felt herself the center of a cyclone. A dozen times already she had feverishly manipulated her recorder to take dictation at a breath-taking speed. Her new employer dictated as he talked, apparently without thought, or, she made the mental note, discretion. For minutes on end he had discussed vast projects on which he was engaged, switching from one business to another with bewildering rapidity; and always the only qualification was, "This is for your private information!"

He said now, "It's just a small note this time. Always spell out the name of our company in small letters, but put the word 'limited' in capitals. There have been some darned funny court rulings on that limited business on the Ridge Star planets. For instance, once it was held that using small letters made the word 'limited' appear insignificant beside a really grand sounding company name. Abbreviating it puts you out of court so fast you won't even know what hit your bank account. Some people will tell you that this is an age of science, but they're wrong—"

It took a moment for Evana to realize that he had changed the subject. She blinked, then adjusted, as Blord rambled on at high speed, "They're wrong because the great

14

developments today are not in science, but in the use of discovered science. People are constantly amazed that I have no science degrees. I'm really the lucky one. I couldn't tell you the electronic structure of more than half a dozen atomettes, or the composition of half a dozen chemical compounds. But I know something far better than that: I know what those things do, and what their relation is to human beings and human progress. I consider myself a sort of super-co-ordinator."

It was his boasting that ended all her fear. There was, of course, the possibility that he was talking about himself and his merits in an objective fashion, and it even seemed probable that he'd be nice in spite of the conceit if she ever got to know him. But the pressure of fear that was on her mind didn't leave room for immediate interest in any man. There was only her necessary purpose. And, thank God, he was guileless and unsuspicious. In a minute now, she'd bring out her cigarettes and—what was he saying? Cigarettes! Would she have a cigarette?

Evana felt briefly startled, then, "I have my own, thank you," she said.

On Blord's desk the needle attached to the chair in which the girl sat was jumping erratically. Doped cigarettes, he thought cynically. And to think he'd been fishing around for an hour expecting something infinitely more subtle. He'd known the moment the girl entered his office that something was wrong. All the thousands of hours he had spent training himself to be what he was concentrated into the first glance he gave her, and revealed that she was mentally nervous without any physical byproducts. That meant a dose of Nonchalant at a hundred stellors a gram. Would an immigrant have that kind of money? Not normally.

The rest was merely a matter of trying to find out who was behind her. And yet all the names he mentioned scarcely stirred the needle. Either she didn't know, or the time had come for more direct action. "Earth cigarettes!" he said eagerly. "Would you mind letting me have one? I sometimes long for them."

He walked around his desk over to the girl. She manipulated the ejector and brought forth two cigarettes. She took the inner one, then held the other out to him. He took it without question. She accepted the light he offered. He walked back to his chair as if forgetting his own cigarette and sat idly holding it between his fingers. The needle, he saw grimly, was hovering around its zenith.

He smiled finally, put the cigarette to his lips, picked up the lighter, stared for a moment at its flame—and with his foot pressed the lever that activated the energy of the chair in which the girl sat. She crumpled like a child falling asleep.

"—listen Doc," he was saying into his phone a few minutes later, "I know it's past two, but I want you up here immediately. I've got a girl whom I want examined physically and mentally, the full hypnotism treatment if necessary. I want her in such a keyed-up condition that she'll be able to look at pictorial records of all the big operators I have had anything to do with in the past year, and be able to recognize them even if she only saw them previously with masks on. I've got to find out who's gunning for me."

It took about an hour for the tests, but when they were over, he had the information he wanted. Doc Gregg dimmed the strong lights that had blazed so long on the girl's unconscious body. And Blord, staring silently, savagely down at her, thought: "The men who would do this to an innocent youngster deserve death in its worst form." He laughed finally, without humor.

Aloud, he said: "There isn't any sense me getting stirred up about this. I know of no way to stop the use of sex dope and the seven-day poison. They fit in too perfectly with the lusts of men. And in a universe of a billion planets, who can ever find the underground factories where the damned stuff is made?"

The old man was staring at him thoughtfully. Doc Gregg said, "Why don't you try hiring men secretaries?"

Blord shook his head. "Men who come to the Ridge Stars are too ambitious to be good employees. I've tried it twice. A fellow called Ganelson who sold information about my operations to the Munar I mining people and made himself enough money to start up as an operator on one of the Gildal planets. The other man couldn't bear the thought of all the money I was making and tried to shoot me. You see," he went on, frowning, "men regard themselves as my competitors; women do not. I've had women angry with me because I didn't want to marry them, but not one has ever tried to do me harm. That may be a callous way of looking at it, but it's the truth."

His dark gaze played over the still form of Evana. "This the first case of a girl being foisted on me with criminal intent. But it merely proves that my habit of hiring only secretaries fresh from Earth, because of their ingrained sense of loyalty, has been found out, and that I'd better investigate the powers behind the Fair Play Employment Agency." He broke off, smiled grimly. "So it's Delaney, Gorder, Dallans, Cansy, Neek and I have no doubt, the rest of the ninety-four competitors for the prize being offered for the new space drive, who are behind this attack. I knew I'd shock them when I entered the competition two weeks ago. After all the money they've spent on research, to have somebody enter who has a reputation for never losing—but I can honestly say this time my conscience is clear. I'm doing it entirely for the good of the Ridge Stars." He smiled again, wryly. "Almost entirely."

"What's the dope on that space drive, anyway?" Doc Gregg asked.

"My usual method," Blord laughed. "I played bullish on human genius and bear on human nature. You may not believe this, but my research laboratories didn't do a stroke of work prior to a month or so ago. And yet we've got the winning drive."

The old man's shrewd gray eyes were staring at him gravely. "I'm not going to guess what you're up to, young man. But it looks as if you've cut into a hornet's nest. What about this kid? She's got five days to live. Any bets that they try to save her if she doesn't deliver the goods?"

"I wouldn't even bet they'd save her if she did," Blord

snapped. He scowled. "Damn it, I can't carry the world on my shoulders. I feel sorry for her, but her only hope is for me to let them capture me as they planned. The worst of it is, they'll be waiting at the Skal's castle on Delfi I. It's the only place such a group could meet. They can't trust each other, but they can all trust the Skal so long as they operate within *his* code. If I thought there was one chance in five, I might risk being the guest of the Skal, but not—"

He stopped. His eyes narrowed with the sudden thought that came. He grew aware finally that the old medico was watching him with a grin. Doc Gregg said softly:

"What do you want me to do, son? Set everything up as it was?"

"Yes," said Blord slowly, "yes. It's that damned instinct of mine for playing with fire. To begin with, I'll need some preconditioning."

Evana had a sense of faintness, that was all. Then she straightened; and there was Artur Blord still lighting the cigarette. She stared at him in fascination as he took a deep puff with evident enjoyment. She cringed inwardly as a startled expression leaped into his eyes.

He half-slid, half-fell to the floor and lay there face up, the ceiling light glowing down on his closed eyes. In that quiet repose the noble lines of his countenance seemed accentuated. All the sillier aspects of him, the volubility, the immense and casual indiscretions, the braggadocio faded and were lost in that physical tranquility. He looked like Adonis struck down by the killer-boar, like a man already dead, needing only a coffin to seal him forever from life.

It was funny, Evana thought shakily, looking down at him, how she had really known all the time that she couldn't sacrifice anyone to save herself. Funny how she had known, too, deep in her mind, that only the ultimate moment would bring her face to face with that reality. Stunned, she sank down in her chair and buried her face in her hands. After several minutes Artur Blord stood up and said gently:

"Thanks, Miss Travis. Your action in a crisis makes me

very glad I decided to try to save you. But now, you've got to go through with it. Listen—"

He was still talking seven minutes later when the warning buzzer sounded. By the time Delaney's men entered the room he was once more in a deep trance state. Three of them carried Blord aboard the spaceship that had landed on the roof of the building. Evana followed silently, almost without awareness of the firm grip the fourth man had on her arm. Blord, lying on a narrow bunk, felt the brief strain as the ship launched upward toward Delfi I.

Chapter 4

The Skal's castle stood on a mountain top on the dead moon that was the companion planet of Delfi II. Remnants of a forgotten civilization, its scores of towers pierced the heavens like gigantic swords. No man had ever penetrated into all its labyrinthian depths, for men entered that antique place only by permission of the one living relic of its long-dead builders: by permission of the Skal.

And it wasn't just because men were being polite, either, Blord remembered grimly. Several attempts had been made by Ridge Star governments to smash the structure, to end a particularly hideous form of white-slave traffic. But atomic energy washed from the alien towers like water spraying over steel. The great doors remained impervious to energy blows of a billion units. Patrol ships, commissioned to prevent pleasure seekers from entering the castle had a habit of disappearing, never to be heard from again. And long ago the Skal had let it be known that the castle was a safe meeting place, at a price, for men who couldn't otherwise trust themselves together.

The ship was slowing. Blord grew tense as, somewhere ahead and outside, there was a rattle of metal, a dull roar that ended as swiftly as it began. The ship moved forward. Then stopped. The rattle of metal sounded once more, vibrantly, behind the ship this time. They were, Blord thought tensely, inside the Castle, and he was committed irrevocably. He lay, eyes closed as tight as ever, but his body was quivering now. He hadn't long to wait.

Something, a strange, unwholesome something, touched against his mind. He had expected it. The stories he had heard had even described what it was like, this mind reading by the Skal, but the actuality was staggering. He lay struggling to suppress his horror, and keep his mind quiet as a visualization transferred from the Skal being to him, a visualization of a long, scaly, reptile body crouching in some nether darkness, peering into his brain with a glee that could have no human counterpart. The Skal was projecting an image of itself. And the picture clung. The reptilian mind studied him, and finally sent a caressing, steely thought:

"You puzzle me, Artur Blord, for you are not unconscious, as you pretend. Yet you have come to my old abode, from which none can escape unless my clients will it. I shall watch the unfolding of the plan in your mind, and shall not betray it. But no force of yours, whether by impulse of the agony of the moment or deep-seated will, shall prevail."

Blord made an intense effort, sent a thought straight at the reptile image. "I'll pay you double, treble, what they are paying."

It seemed to Blord then that laughter entered soundlessly into his mind; and finally there came a satirical thought:

"Would you seduce the honor of my house? Know then that today and always my loyalty and my protection go to those who have my Castle in their tenure. Such is my code." Again the soundless laughter came. "So shall it be, ever—or at least until I cease to find delight in the antics of those who seek the safety that is here."

Blord snarled, mentally, "Go to hell, you *damned* thing." Almost, he said it aloud. But the mind, the image, was withdrawing, still giving vent to its unnatural laughter. Simultaneously—and that was what stopped his words—hands grabbed him out of the bunk.

A voice said, "Lay him on the gravitor roller. Keep Travis on board. The boss'll take care of her later."

There was a hiss of air locks opening, and then the gravitor began to move. It seemed to be rolling along a glass-smooth floor. The pressure of light on Blord's eyelids shadowed noticeably. Very carefully, and for the first time, he parted them slightly. He was in a dim tunnel gliding along faster than he had thought. The dully lighted surface of the roof sliding by, seemed to emit a reflection of some remoter light rather than itself being a source. Abruptly, the tunnel widened, opened up into a large round room. Blord had a swift impression of human shapes in semi-darkness. The next instant the gravitor slowed. As it pulled to a stop, a man's voice said somewhere out of the darkness:

"Ah, our guest has arrived." Then: "Waken him!"

Blord sat up. He had no desire to have the unpleasant revival drug injected into his system. These doped cigarettes were not expected to have a lasting effect, so his return to consciousness should not cause too much suspicion. A few doubts, however, wouldn't matter. He peered around him; then, "Good God!" he said. He mustn't overdo his surprise, he thought, but a little frank bewilderment would not be out of place.

He saw that a radium bulb, turned dead slow, lay on or protruded from the middle of the floor. A ghostly luminescence came from it and it was by that dim radiance that the outlines of men were visible. The masks the men wore added an inhuman quality to the scene, that ended as the shape that had already spoken said, "I don't think we need delay. We are all busy men and there can be no doubt in the minds of any of us as to the purpose of this meeting." His voice was mocking as he finished, "I'm sure even Mr. Blord understands."

Blord shook his head. "I'm damned if I do," he said flatly. His tone became aggrieved, "And I think I have a right . . ."

21

The masked man interrupted him coldly. "A man who is about to die can have no rights. Mr. Blord, you have meddled in the affairs of others for the last time. We are tired of your superclever tricks, and of your interfering with the profits of honest men. But enough of this. As I have said, we are all aware of our purpose here, but for the sake of our guest, let me recapitulate.

"As you know, when Interstellar, subsidiary of the Galactic Company, believing its space drive patents made its position invincible, asked prohibitive rates and impossible preliminary fees to start an organized passenger and transport service in the Ridge Star system, our governments announced an open competition. They had purchased local rights to a drive vastly inferior to the Galactic drive, and asked competitors to put their research staffs to the task of improving it. All improvements were guaranteed to the companies that made them, and in the event of a duplication, an equitable adjustment was promised."

"Pardon me," Blord interrupted. "But has anyone developed a drive that's as much as one quarter as fast as the Galactic? If not, then every person in this meeting is cutting his own financial throat."

'What do you mean?' said a voice.

"Never mind what he means!" roared the man who was standing. "Can't you see he's trying to start us arguing?"

"I mean," Blord cut in swiftly, "that a property pays according to the speed with which produced goods are transferred to market. The only reason I entered the contest was that I heard of some of the ridiculously low speeds that—"

"Shut up!"

Blord shrugged. He had put over his first point. It was one that had undoubtedly occurred previously to them all, but it could stand stressing. The speaker was continuing:

"Two weeks ago, with a great fanfare, and a flourish of publicity, Artur Blord entered the competition. What had been a serious and expensive business enterprise became a circus." Bitterness crept into the man's voice. "Such is the fantastic reputation of this man that the ninety-four companies which had spent billions of stellors on research were instantly made laughingstocks, pitied by newspaper editors, butts for fools, comedians, pranksters. And there is, of course, no doubt that Blord, knowing his fame, knew also that he could not afford a failure. Therefore, we assumed that he had the prize-winning drive, and, through the Skal, someone called the first meeting, where a plan for getting Mr. Blord here was agreed upon. I was selected by lot to carry it out. Our purpose is to obtain from Mr. Blord the secret of his drive, and to force him to sign over to us all rights to his ship."

"Is it possible," Blord said, "that the great individualistic operators of the Ridge Stars have at last agreed to co-operate, even if it is only a division of spoils that is involved? However, I'm sorry, but you're all too late."

"What do you mean?"

"I have already assigned my rights to the Delfi Government, to take effect in the event that I do not turn up at the contest, with the stipulation that a public utility be formed. As for getting the secret out of me, that's impossible. Purely by accident I had myself counterhypnotized today, and by some odd coincidence it was about this very matter."

"What?"

The shout was followed by a dead silence that developed into a restless shuffling of bodies. At last a voice said softly:

"At least we can still kill him. At least we can prevent him from being a damned nuisance to us in the future."

Chapter 5

Blord climbed slowly from the gravitor. He realized for the first time as his feet touched the hard floor that he was not, as he had always believed, a brave man. The weakness in his knees made him feel faint and unsteady. And when he spoke, he had difficulty in keeping a tremor out of his voice. He said:

"You seem to have me gentlemen. But I would say that you should think twice before you kill me. When I get into traps like this, I am usually prepared to make a deal."

"The rat's beginning to squeal," somebody sneered from the darkness.

Blord shrugged. The fear was gone now. "As I understand it," he said coolly, "the two main complaints against me are that I have endangered research investments and that I have made you all the subject of ridicule. It seems to me that if everyone's investment is guaranteed and the ridicule is turned on me, you gain—"

A voice exploded, "Is this the great Artur Blord talking, or a louse?

There was a general murmur of disgust. In spite of himself, Blord flushed at the intensity of their sudden contempt. He knew the codes that governed these far-flung frontiers of space, and he could visualize how his words would later be broadcast to shame him. The thought put sharpness into his tone as he snapped:

"Hear my proposition at least. It's to your advantage."

"Oh, sure," said a scathing voice. "Let's hear his proposition. The shock is over now."

Blord felt a quaver of intense irritation at these men who could use sex-dope on innocent women, seven-day poison, murder and straight robbery as instruments of their will without a qualm, but who felt so strongly about any show of physical cowardice. With an effort he fought down his anger. The code was there. It existed. He hadn't figured it into his plan, but the very strength of their feelings on the subject made everything easier.

"My ship," he began, "will win the race. It has attained a speed just under eighty-one percent of a Galactic liner. If anyone can equal that, just let him speak now, and I'll go quietly to the slaughterhouse. Well?" He paused, then went on, sardonically, "I am prepared to make the following offer, to be drawn up immediately, signed and sealed:

"That a joint stock company be formed with an issue of two hundred shares. Of these, fifty shall belong to me. One share each shall be assigned to each of ninety-three of the ninety-four companies, on the condition that they sign over all their patent rights to the new firm.

"The other fifty-seven shares shall be turned over to Seldon Delaney, who will operate the company under the Kallear Regulations.

"I must be released immediately after the signing.

"Evana Travis shall be given the antidote and turned over to me unharmed at once.

"Anyone or group may launch all the ridiculing propaganda they care to against me.

"The whole agreement is nullified unless I am alive at the time of the contest, and it goes into effect only if my ship does in fact win the prize."

A man shouted, "This will ruin you, Blord. The lowest riffraff will despise you after we get through publicizing how much dirt you've eaten."

Artur Blord shrugged, but made no comment. He waited only long enough to be sure that the documents would, in fact, be drawn up, then he left the room and walked along a dim-lit corridor. At a little distance along it, he found a standard eldophone from which he put in a call for one of his own ships to come and pick him up. For some time then, he wandered down the dank corridors of the Skal's castle. It was his first visit to the age-musty place, and he was curious. He assumed the Skal would bar him from any part of the interior it didn't want him to intrude upon.

. . . Cavelike corridors, dimly lighted, rooms that had evidently been remodeled for human beings. Bedrooms, living quarters, a restaurant, people— He shook his head in wonder, but spoke to no one. Several times he came to blank walls which had the appearance of having been recently constructed.

Amid all the dampness, and dimness, there was no sign of

the Skal himself. Blord returned, finally, to the "conference" room, and affixed his signature to all the copies after glancing through each in turn.

It was three hours after that that his spaceship flashed down to pick him up. And it was then, as he was stepping out of one of the dim tunnels of the Castle into the bright interior of the machine, that he felt the unpleasant touching against his mind that was the thought of the Skal.

"Well done, Artur Blord. How they will howl when their ridicule recoils upon them. Your ingenuity has given an unexpected titillation to my old nerves. To show my appreciation of such an intellectual delicacy, you may call upon me at any time for one favor. Good luck."

"But what is your plan?" Evana asked blankly, as the ship hurtled through space. "You said you had one. But all that I can see is that you're going to lose your reputation and you've signed away seventy-five percent of your rights to the winning space drive."

She looked genuinely bewildered. Blord stared at her thoughtfully, then he flung back his head and laughed. "Don't forget, I didn't even have a space drive three weeks ago," he said. "And what mainly interests me is that the Ridge Stars get a fast transport. But of course, once I had thought of it, the idea was too lovely to let go by default."

Evana was persistent. "But what was the idea?"

"Very simple, I was convinced that after the contest there would be a merging of all the best ideas presented in the contesting space drives. I anticipated, that's all. It cost me large sums in bribery, but I bought the research results of all the entries, and had my own technicians combine the best features of several of them. You see," he finished blandly, "when they discover that they've signed away their own patent rights, that *they*, in fact, provided the drive, I don't think they'll feel like laughing any more."

Evana said, "But that awful Mr. Delaney! Why did you make him—"

Blord interrupted. "He had you and he had the antidote to the poison. Don't forget that. I had no choice; and don't think he didn't know it. I had to let him have charge of the new interstellar drive, and so naturally he had to be made head of the company that will use it."

There was a long silence, then Evana said in a small voice: "What about me?"

Blord looked at her quizzically; then he smiled. "I really do need a secretary," he said. "Do you think you'd like the job?"

Chapter 6

It was a normal day for the vast city of Suderea, not too warm, not too cool. The buildings glowed in the sunlight. And Evana Travis, walking along Financial Avenue during the lunch hour one day of her sixth month with Artur Blord, glanced into every gleaming shop window, and thrilled to the sense of excitement that quivered in the air.

People hurried past her as if bent on some joyful mission. That was the wonderful thing about the planets of the stars that formed the curious deformation in space known as the Ridge. They infected people with the germs of eagerness and expectancy. And then fulfilled their highest hopes. At least, it seemed that way to Evana.

She felt jaunty and very much at ease as she swung through the giant double doors of the Blord Building. The two smartly uniformed men who had opened the doors for her grinned at her in friendly fashion. Their friendliness added to her feeling of well-being, and she smiled back at them as she went with quickened step toward the elevators.

When she reached the penthouse floor, she found herself tingling with excitement. It was a feeling often with her these past three weeks—a wonder if *today* Artur Blord would return, might even now be in his office.

The thought sent her hurrying along the corridor. In a flutter of expectancy she flung open the door of her apartment and sniffed the air eagerly. But there was no telltale whiff of the special brand of cigarette that was always such a sure sign of his presence.

Less eagerly now, she crossed to the door leading to the office suite. It, too, was empty. She was turning to re-enter her apartment when the eldophone on the wall above her desk rang loudly. And this time she was not disappointed.

Artur Blord said, "I've been trying to get in touch with you."

"I went out for lunch today," Evana said. "And for a walk."

"Just a moment, Evana, " Blord interrupted. "I've got warning signals coming in. I'll call you again later."

He waited until Evana's face disappeared from the plate, then he turned to the control board.

METAL! flashed the automatic alarms of the spaceship control board. METAL! METAL!

Artur Blord peered into the plates, frowning, but there was only darkness in the direction the pointers were indicating. Darkness, and a faint sprinkling of stars. A quick glance at the estimator showed that he was three light-years from the Zand sun, and eight from the double star, Carox A and B, the next nearest of the Ridge Star suns.

Could be an iron meteorite, he thought. But not very likely. Not out here. Besides, his automatics were of the advanced Rejector type. They could examine any simple structure such as a meteor, adjust to its course, and proceed at top speed, all without sounding an alarm.

A ship then? Blord sent a quick glance at the power recorder, but the instrument showed no sign of life. Whatever was out there wasn't manufacturing enough energy to heat a radiator, let alone drive a coil.

Nothing like being nosey, he thought wryly. But he knew it was more than that. The odd quality in his character that made him curious about anything and everything, the quality that enabled him to withdraw his entire attention from an

28

important transaction and become absorbed in something seemingly completely irrelevant and immaterial, had made him the despair of his associates and the wonder of his enemies.

With a flick of his hand he touched the button that synchronized his telescopic cameras with the glowing pointers, and pressed home the plunger. The yellow tracers leaped into view on the plate. Though slower than light, they reached it almost instantly. The photographs showed a spaceship about a fifth of a mile long. Evidently, it was coasting along on a course that was almost precisely parallel with his own, or it would not still be in range, not at the velocity he was travelling. In the ever increasing space traffic, such accidental interception had become possible. Blord snapped on his eldophone. "Vision call!" he intoned into the mouthpiece. "Vision call!"

There was no answer. A derelict, he thought, and sent his memory rapidly back over the list of spaceship accidents that had occurred in the Ridge Stars since his own arrival fifteen years before. Not counting those caught in the dead zone of the Lorelei sun, it was a scanty list and they had all been recovered. In no case, he remembered, had there been any doubt about the cause of the disaster. And the pattern had never varied. All the men dead, all the women missing.

Suddenly grim, he maneuvered toward the ship. As he had expected, the locks hung open; the temperature on the thermometer of his spacesuit registered forty below, centigrade, as he moved along the corridor from his point of entrance, splitting the darkness with the glaring lights from his headpiece. About two hours, he thought. It would take that long for the ship's interior to cool.

He came to his first dead body. It was of a man, a fine-looking chap, whose left breast had been shot away by what, from the size of the wound, could only have been a semimoble blaster. There were other dead bodies as Blord hurried along, all men, some of them horribly mutilated by the ravenous energy that had smashed them. His anger grew into rage, and as always that made him more, not less, alert. It was the alertness that saved him.

He had opened a tightly closed door, felt the air rush past him, and he was peering in when it happened, a movement glimpsed from the corner of his left eye. A movement with enough menace in it to send him diving for the floor. The splash of the hand blaster sprayed the air where he had been. Instantly, Blord was on his feet. The energy was still coruscating on the far wall when he had the arm that wielded the gun—had the wielder bent backward over his knee, helpless. He looked down into a woman's face wet with tears of panic-stricken terror, blue with cold, and already gasping for breath.

She thawed out in the warming environment of Blord's ship. The fear that had seemed a part of her facial structure, scaled off like a horror mask removed. Underneath was a distinctive face, and a personality that seemed to recover quickly from the shattering blows it had been dealt. She looked around with bright blue eyes. "This is a private space yacht?" she asked.

Blord nodded. But he did not take his gaze from her. He was puzzled. The freighter had been a spaceship from Earth, loaded with a human cargo for the Ridge Stars. Usually, the girls and women aboard such vessels were relatively innocent, filled with wide-eyed eagerness, products of a crimeless planet. This woman didn't quite fit. She had a delicate, youthful, almost girlish face, but after a moment he did not hesitate to assess her age at thirty.

The woman quickly tired of her examination of her surroundings. The excitement of the rescue was beginning to wear off, and there was weariness in her eyes and in her voice. "I'm Ellen Reith. I suppose you want to know what happened."

Blord shook his head. "I know what happened," he said. "We'll talk about it later. Right now, I think you'd better get some rest."

"You *know* what happened!" Her blue eyes were wide.

"Then you know who's responsible, and where the other women were taken."

Blord nodded.

Ellen Reith stared at him. "Where?"

Blord sighed. He could appreciate the fascination the fate she had escaped would have on her. When he had told her, she lay very quiet. Her body seemed taut under the blanket he had placed over her. She whispered finally, "You mean men actually do that," she gestured as though toward the ravaged space freighter, "and kill all the male passengers, just to get women for this Skal's Castle? Why doesn't the Space Patrol stop it?" Her voice went higher. "You've reported what happened, haven't you?"

"Well, no," Blord said slowly. "Not exactly. Not yet."

"But," she gasped urgently, "there may be others aboard, alive. And perhaps the ship with the women can be intercepted. They—" She seemed to realize that her words were hardly touching him. With a convulsive effort, she pulled herself back out of the hysteria, and said sharply, "What's wrong with doing something? What's wrong with trying to save others who are aboard?"

"Go to sleep!" said Blord. He stood up and walked out of the little room, back to the control board. He was convinced that his examination of the ravaged freighter had been thorough. No one remained alive aboard it. He had made a point of leaving everything exactly as he found it; the bodies in their sprawled positions, the air locks open. Beyond doubt it had been a job done with the assistance of men who had come with the freighter all the way from Earth. An inside job carried out with clocklike precision at a set rendezvous by the gangs of human scum who were the present tenants of the home of that sardonic and ancient beast, the Skal.

Six months ago, the Skal had promised him a favor. But Blord knew that it would never grant any favor that endangered the men who used his house. They were now endangered. Because of the physical examinations regulating people who emigrated to the stars, they'd have to be aboard undisguised. By this time they knew that a woman had escaped

31

them. A woman who must have seen some of the gang aboard the freighter. A woman, accordingly, who would be destroyed unless he took every conceivable counteraction.

He put his calls through, but it was two hours before his eldophone *brred* softly. The first reply was from his business manager, Magrusson. The plump man spoke softly, as if the subject matter had a subduing effect on him:

"The invisible ship will meet you five hours from now. The pilot will be Nicer, who will make the exchange above the jungle island of Carox A II, and will then proceed here, where he will be conditioned to believe that he was the one who actually took your ship out from Zand."

Blord said doubtfully, "I guess that's the best we can do. I don't know just how such a conditioning would hold up if he were taken before the Skal. I have an idea, from my own experience, that it can go deeper into minds than any covering up we can do. It's important to remember, however, that it may take no part in the game at all. It probably holds itself aloof, an observer rather than participant. I'm simply taking no unnecessary chances. If you think of any further precautions on your own, let me know."

The second call came a few minutes later. Evana's face flashed onto the plate. "Mr. Blord," she said swiftly, "I went in and talked to the chief of the Secret Police of the Patrol as you suggested. I didn't tell him, of course, why I wanted the information. I pretended that I had just come across a piece about it. Well, he opened right up."

"Good girl!"

Evana smiled with pleasure at the praise, then grew more serious. "I'm afraid you're out of luck if you're really planning to tackle the Skal, unless you can get the beast to kill itself as a special favor to you and to Delfi II."

"Maybe you've got something there," Blord laughed softly. "It does owe me a favor. But go on. What's wrong?"

"Everything! You wanted information as to the various attacks made on the Castle by the Ridge Star governments. Well, I went down to the laboratory and asked Marian Clark about it. She was able to give me the details, and here they are: The castle is made of a metal, or is a force structure, that doesn't even start to fuse when atomic energy is directed against it. As you know, there were other ancient buildings at one time on Delfi I, relics of a civilization of long-dead Skal. They were all destroyed rather suddenly soon after human beings came to Delfi II. But not before some loose pieces had been taken to Earth for study.

"Nobody knows what the metal is. It's the old trouble: Age hardening of alloys using catalysts. Unless you know the catalytic agent and the environment, method and period of hardening, you can study the finished metal until your mind congeals without learning its secrets. The metal's electronic pattern is known. Marian will send you the formula. And that's all about that. But here's something very special and private:

"Ninety-six police warships were destroyed in the three attacks made on the Castle. That's never been revealed publicly. They were destroyed by a bright green ray, the electronic structure of which was similar in every detail to that of the metal. Figure that one out—says Marian.

"Finally, here's the data on the other hide-outs of the men who use the Skal's Castle. There are so many suns, so many unexplored planets that even looking for hideaways seems hopeless. But it's obvious that they must have supply centers in big cities. Two places are under strong suspicion. One is the great Midnight Club in the city Negor on Fasser III; the other—"

"Just a minute," Blord cut in. "I'll get those names recorded."

When he had them, his tone changed. "How's everything with you, Evana?"

Evana flashed him a brilliant smile. "Just wonderful, Mr. Blord. But I wish you wouldn't stay away from Delfi II so much. Mr. Magrusson has got just stacks of papers for you to sign."

Blord laughed. "Poor Magrusson. Frankly, I don't think he'd be happy if he didn't have those 'stacks' of unsigned documents to worry about. And don't you worry about me.

I'll be home soon, now. In fact, I was on my way when I ran into this thing. Take care of yourself, Evana."

Evana said, "Good-by, Mr. Blord." And the plate went dark.

Blord turned, then stopped and stared thoughtfully at Ellen Reith. She was sitting in a chair ten feet away, and she looked as if she had been there for several minutes at least. Her short sleep had had a revivifying effect; and she had found time to do neat things to her dark brown hair. Her eyes sparkled. Slim and self-possessed, she sat eyeing him, a faint smile on her delicate, aristocratic face. The smile became a shadow.

"I heard it all, except part of the man's words, enough to gather that I'm in danger. Is that right?"

She didn't look as if she were afraid. Two hours before she had seemed thirty. Now Blord found himself gazing at her admiringly. He liked mature women who could look eighteen under stress. And, as he had never intended to keep her in the dark, he explained the situation briefly. When he had finished, the woman was silent for a long moment. Finally, she said irrelevantly, "Who is she?" She waved at the eldoplate.

Blord stood up and stared down at her, a mocking smile crinkling his lips. "Think of her," he said slowly, "as one whose information might save your life *if* we can think of some way to use it."

For a long time after that, there was silence, Blord said finally, "Miss Reith——" he paused, then——"It is 'Miss,' I presume."

Ellen Reith nodded. "Reith is my own name. I've had a number of others. I was married the first time at seventeen." She contemplated the toes of her shoes for several seconds, then she looked up with candid eyes. "I made an awful mess of my life back there—too much money and too few responsibilities can do that, you know. I've come out here to make a new start." She laughed, wryly. "I intend to marry a farmer, have five children and pretend there never was such a person as Mrs. Gilmour-Morgan-Davis-Castlefield."

Blord said, "That's quite an impressive list of names."

She shrugged, but didn't answer. And Blord realized the confession was complete. He sat watching her for some seconds, then he said briskly, "In a few minutes we'll be changing ships, and we have a few preparations to make. We may as well be ready."

Chapter 7

The transfer to the invisible ship took place in midair over restless gray waters near an island. The pilot Nicer neither saw nor suspected the presence of a woman. Clothed in a roomy invisibility suit, she slipped aboard the larger, more luxurious vessel while Blord talked rapidly to the pilot. Then he followed the woman aboard, and Nicer entered the yacht. Swiftly, the two ships withdrew from their lonely rendezvous, and plunged in opposite directions toward distant suns.

After an hour, Ellen Reith had still not appeared from her quarters which she had found without assistance. She probably needed more sleep. It was time he had a nap himself. He set the automatics, and connected the alarms to his cabin. When he awoke, fully refreshed, the ship was still hurtling toward its remote objective. He took a leisurely shower, and dressed slowly, his mind occupied with nothing more important than the food he would find in the galley.

Ellen Reith's door remained closed. But somebody had been in the galley and neglected to put the dishes in the Beldex. Blord smiled, as the possibility struck him that she did not even know how to operate an automatic dish-washing machine. It was a pretty tribute to civilization.

He ate thoughtfully, then examined the wire for messages. But there was nothing. Vaguely disappointed, he busied himself with some papers that Magrusson had thoughtfully piled high in a case labeled URGENT BUSINESS. Blord smiled over the documents. Magrusson kept papers to be signed strategically spread throughout the Ridge Stars. There was special offices that, under radio supervision, did nothing but type original copies. As soon as any one of these was signed, all other copies were destroyed, wherever they might be. The development of the system that fitted so beautifully in with his own casual character still made Blord feel appreciative.

He sat down and applied himself to his task. He was aware once that the woman came out of her apartment and went into the galley, then disappeared into her suite without a word. Finally, weary himself, Blord dumped the still enormous pile of unsigned and unread documents into their case. He ate a second meal, and there was still nothing on the wire. Yawning widely, he returned to his cabin and was swiftly in a sound sleep.

This time, when he awoke, there were three messages on the wire, all from Magrusson. Blord read them with the exhilarating knowledge that the period of inaction was about to end. The first message read:

A special high-powered, heavily armored ship visited the derelict after nineteen hours. Fought running battle with three police ships, but finally escaped.

The second message said:

The police have issued a bulletin on the ravaged freighter *Crescent Moon*, stating that nine hundred seventy-four bodies were found. One of them, that of a woman, has been identified as Mrs. Gilmour-Morgan-Davis-Castlefield, heiress to the Reith multibillion fortune. The former Miss Reith was described as apparently having hid herself during the attack, but had afterward been frozen to death as she evidently did not know how to close the air locks which had been left open by the marauders.

The third message said:

Nothing yet.

It didn't make sense until he glanced at the time of receipt registered on each message. Blord smiled. The young lady might not be able to operate an automatic dish-washing machine, but she did know about wires. The only thing was, she should have made a point of putting them back in proper time sequence. A sound intruded upon his amusement. Behind him, Ellen Reith said, "But who was the dead woman?"

Blord turned and stared at her. She had selected a very simple dark dress from the wardrobe which one of Magrusson's fantastically priced couturiers had supplied on the basis of eldophoned measurements; but the simpleness was an illusion of style. Her cheeks glowed with skillfully applied color. Her lips were full and red.

Blord said with a shrug: "It was really very simple. I have had need of bodies before; and accordingly, basic arrangements were actually made long ago. It was only a matter of finding among the tens of thousands of available bodies one that approximated yours. Make-up experts did the rest. It was rushed out to the *Crescent Moon* by a ship whose ownership cannot possibly be traced back to me. The pilot returned to his base, secretly informed the police, had all memory of the episode conditioned out of him, and he is now on a liner Earthbound for a year's vacation. He—"

Blord stopped, because the woman was gazing at him with a strange expression. "What's the matter?" he asked.

"You!" she breathed. "What kind of a man are you? You've thought of everything. It's like a dream. It all happened so swiftly, yet you did everything with such an exact skill." She shook her head wonderingly, then slowly the intensity faded. She said anxiously, "I'm safe now, am I?"

"Only if the Skal has not been informed. However," he went on coolly, "I think we are now ready for the attack."

"Attack?"

He nodded. "You don't think," he said coldly, "that I'm

going to let that bloody gang continue to operate unscathed?" He frowned. "What I really need against the Skal is one of my hunches, but until then, the gang is my meat." He gave her a searching look. "I think," he said at last, "you've got the courage. So—"

The Midnight Club occupied the peak of a high hill overlooking the vast city of Negor, of Fasser III. Blord edged the car toward the curb, motioned with his hand.

"Six years ago I stood on this hill and gazed down over this plain toward that dark glittering sea down there. A few tents, a couple of spaceships squatting on the ground unloading machinery, and the tiny figures of several thousand men looking like little scurrying rats was what I saw." He leaned back, then smiled at Ellen Reith. "The city hasn't been built quite as I pictured it then. But the difference is my own fault. I have an unfortunate trait of character which prevents me from taking an interest in the details of an operation once it's started. The result is other men with other dreams wove their patterns. But that's the glory of life in the Ridge Stars. Tens of millions of men each with his own master design for the future come here, and make their own pictures on the living canvas of this part of the universe."

The woman's eyes were glowing. "And the greatest designer of all is Artur Blord." She spoke softly, but her voice was resonant as she went on, "I've been with you for three days, and I'm only just beginning to realize how tremendous is the work you're doing." She broke off: "That woman who gave you all that information about the attacks on the Skal—she's one of your wives, isn't she?"

Blord looked at her, but didn't answer.

She shook her head impatiently. Her eyes were pools of intense blue in the dim light from the instrument board. "You can't fool me. And you've got more women out there, haven't you, who'd rather share one hundreth part of your life than have the full time attention of a whole score of lesser men?"

"Wait!" She cut him off as he attempted to speak. "Don't deny it. You don't have to, not with me. Because it's right.

You know in your heart and in your mind that those women have made no mistake. The universe is too big, too complicated, for little men's children. Each succeeding generation has to be quicker-minded, bolder, stronger. And the cycle must go on faster and faster, as man expands into ten million other galaxies. Life can't wait for old moralities. And the mothers of the race have been the first to realize it. They come out here, innocent, stiff-minded but brave. And in a single leap of comprehension realize their destiny."

Blord was laughing gently. "All this," he marveled, "from a young lady who is going to marry a farmer and have ten kids."

Her laughter echoed his, but there was a note of scorn in it. "What a fool I was! For years I was like a moth, singeing myself in a fire I didn't understand, becoming more bewildered every time I got burned. A dozen times I thought of committing suicide, which only goes to show how tremendous were the forces of which I was so dimly aware." She caught his arm. "Artur Blord," she said, and suddenly she sounded tense, "you must save me. I couldn't bear to die now. There's so much to do, so many things to experience."

Blord reached forward and placed his finger on her lips. "Careful!" he admonished. "That's the wrong attitude. Fear of death is the most dangerous of all phobias out here. One thing you've got to be prepared for is to die any minute." He drew back, stared at her coolly. "You've agreed to visit the Midnight Club with me. In spite of the fact that we're both disguised, the danger is great enough to place considerable strain on the nerves of anyone unaccustomed to such situations. Accordingly, unless you can convince me that—"

Her laughter, amused, unstrained, gently mocking, rippled across his words, and ended as she said earnestly, "I wasn't thinking about myself. You must believe that. It's important that I live because ... because of the things I must do. I don't know just how to describe that but—"

Blord was shaking his head. "Never mind," he said gently. "Those things can't be described. You've told me what I want to know. Let's go. Remember, my name is Chris Delton, and you're Rita Kelly."

Soundlessly, the long car glided forward. A moment later, a club attendant was opening the door. The attendant climbed into the car and drove it toward a parking place. Neither Blord nor the woman so much as glanced back. One by one the glittering doors of the club opened before them and closed behind them. In three minutes they were deep into the interior of the enormous mass of buildings that was the Midnight Club.

Chapter 8

"I'm becoming bewildered," Ellen Reith said after an hour. "I've played games I didn't know existed, and I've made eight hundred thousand stellors. It's silly to be excited, but I can't get used to the idea of so much freedom." She broke off, confessed, "I feel like a child in a brand-new world, and in about two seconds I'm going to wake up."

Blord laughed. "Earth is trying to keep its population. Therefore, practically everything is illegal. There are no easy ways to make money. And, while people are paid good wages, there's a clever method of making them spend their earnings so that only a small percentage of them can ever manage to break away.

"Gambling is bad only when losing might mean poverty or hunger. But that doesn't apply in this universe of high wages, cheap food and so many jobs that employers and would-be employers nearly go crazy outbidding each other for the services of newcomers. The human race has always had a sound emotional instinct as to what pleasure they want. For the first time in history, the lust to build, to create and to enjoy can be experienced simultaneously, not by a few privileged, but by all."

"Then you approve of this club?" Her eyes were wide.

Blord stared at her in surprise. "Why, of course." He smiled. "Don't forget that you can lose that eight hundred thousand as quickly as you won it."

"I don't mean that. I mean the gang behind this club."

Blord frowned and shook his head. "I cannot compare the actions of criminals with the will of a human being to enjoy himself where he pleases after his day's work is done. The former I shall destroy without mercy; the latter, well, when he is having a good time, so is God. That's my religion." He stopped, because he saw that the woman's eyes were intent on something behind him.

"That man!" she whispered. "The one who's talking to the group. He was aboard."

Blord said, "Turn back to your drink. Your eyes are too fixed. Relax!"

She looked at him, and managed a wan smile. "Sorry," she said; then, "But hadn't you better get a look at him so you won't forget his face?"

Blord shook his head, but he made no answer. And he sighed inwardly. It was obvious that Ellen Reith had yet to learn not to offer advice as to what he ought to do long after he had done it.

Blord smiled wryly. But he was not really ashamed of the conceit behind that thought. She should have remembered that she had submitted herself to hypnotism. True, he had deliberately refrained from showing her the hypnotically remembered composite drawings she had made of the faces of several score of carefully selected men. Faces selected on the basis of her mental reaction to them, the instinctive hostility of that deeper brain that could read character at a glance or word. But he had withheld them from her for a purpose. One of the drawings had been of the man whom she had now identified. A man whom Blord had been following for thirty minutes without pointing him out, in order that her final identification be untinged by suggestion of any kind.

He saw that the woman was watching him keenly. She said quickly, "I've said something wrong. Is it possible that I've been moving along quite ignorantly into the very center of one of your intricate plots?"

Blord smiled. "It's possible," he admitted. "Now, here's what you do!" He explained briefly. "I admit this is pretty short notice, and it might put you in a very grave danger. But if this fellow's mind has been conditioned at all, we've got to knock his brains loose, and freeze him while he's off his mental balance."

She was white, but after a moment she mustered a shaky smile. "It's all right. Start your fireworks. I'll take off my mask the moment you reach him."

Blord stood up. "That's the spirit."

Her smile mocked him as he started to turn. She said, "If this is what it takes to become a member of that harem of yours, I intend to pass with double-A honors."

"Don't be an idiot," said Blord rudely. And walked off.

Out of the corner of his eye, Blord saw a dozen of his men casually stroll into position encircling the table where Ellen Reith remained. Others, including some of his women agents, formed in little groups outside the inner circle, creating a second and stronger ring of defense around her. It was the most he could do for her. He turned his attention to the man she had identified.

The man leaned confidently against the crystal bar, talking with animation to five of Blord's agents. As Blord came up, the fellow skillfully included him in the conversation. "I was just telling these gentlemen," he confided, "about my recent visit to the Skal's Castle. There's a brand-new bunch of women up there. It's a little expensive, but you'll never regret a single stellor of it."

It was at that point that Blord stepped up to the panderer and said in an undertone, "Cut it, fellow! And take a look at the woman at the table over there. The boss wants to know whether you know her."

"Huh!" ejaculated the man. "You're not one of u—" He stopped. Involuntarily, he turned to look. The color drained from his cheeks. "But she's dead!" he gasped. "The police said—"

He stopped again. But this time it was involuntary, as Blord pressed the activator of a very curious instrument. An instrument which, when synchronized with its recorder, strapped to the body of Blord's assistant who had taken up a position behind the victim, sent nerve energy pouring up a million nerve paths, and, like a solvent, loosened the thoughts, shocked through areas of resistance and, with particular violence, flushed everything that connected with the idea forms that had been in the mind at the moment it was applied. Its effect was cumulative, and the peak body of confession would not begin to pour forth until some two hours after the dose of energy was taken. After that its potency declined rapidly. Though basically harmless, its manufacture was a government monopoly, and its private use prohibited under severe penalty.

It was one of the hundreds of expensive devices Blord had gathered into what, for want of a better name, he called his coordination department. With a bland conviction Blord believed that, while there were millions of people who knew how one or a few of the thousands of devices worked, only he, who knew little of the details of construction, had ever co-ordinated so many inventions to a single pattern of action evolving out of one brain. Blord said now, coolly, "Let's go out into the garden, and you can tell me the details!"

A brain that could only acquiesce to every suggestion had no resistance to that. But Blord had to hold the man's elbow to keep him from staggering drunkenly. They reached the terrace, and walked to the dark end of the garden below, where the first of the two invisible ships waited. It rose the moment Blord and his prisoner entered.

Blord verified that the second ship was on the point of landing in the garden, then forgot about it. Five hours later, he emerged, smiling with satisfaction, from the laboratory on Delfi II. "So," he said to Evana Travis, "the master minds hold a meeting every two months in the Midnight Club, and the next meeting is scheduled for two weeks from tonight.

And now," he finished, "did you arrange accommodation for Miss Reith for tonight. And by the way, where is she?"

"Hasn't come yet." Evana looked puzzled. "It's funny, too. They should really have arrived a couple of hours ago."

"When she comes," Blord began, "tell her—" His voice trailed into silence. He had been lowering himself into the chair before his desk. Now he straightened. "WHAT?" he yelled.

The eldophone on his desk flickered with the blue light of an interstellar call. Blord waved vaguely at it. "Answer it," he muttered. He walked over to a window, whispered huskily, "I ought to be shot, pitting myself against the Skal. If anything has happened to her—"

He found himself listening with puzzled attention to what Evana was saying into the eldophone. Then, with a swift movement, he walked over and took the instrument from her extended hand. Savagely, he said into the mouthpiece, "You can't fool me. The Skal is incapable of human speech."

There was a chuckle from the earphone that brought a chill. The chuckle ended and a mechanical voice said:

"For such calls as this, Artur Blord, I use an instrument which translates thoughts into language. After all, there is a very compact similar instrument in existence in your head. Would you doubt that I am capable of solving the comparatively simple physical energy problems involved?"

He doubted nothing. The whole thing was very clear to him. The questions that remained were: How had the Skal found out? and why was it calling now? He said jerkily, "Get to the point."

The chilling chuckle came again. "Is it possible, Mr. Blord, that my high regard for you is not reciprocated? I have watched with admiration your remarkable efforts to conceal the fact that Ellen Reith is alive. I can say frankly and honestly that I couldn't have done better myself under similar circumstances."

"Look!" Blord began, but the voice went on insistently, ignoring the interruption.

"To begin with, my investigation was of a routine nature. I

44

was interested in the identity of all ships and pilots known to be within several star distances of the derelict. I was interested in discovering how the fingerprints of the dead woman's body compared with those of Ellen Reith. Naturally, these and similar inquiries took a little time, but not too long, not too long, Mr. Blord. I refused, as you would no doubt have done in my position, to accept the apparent picture as evidence, and so by the end of the third sidereal day—"

Blord interrupted in a flat voice, "What have you done with her and my agents? What do you want?"

The answer was a harsh sound of amusement, then the inhuman voice came again, "How impatient we are! My victory, as you must realize, is sharply qualified. I am in the very peculiar position of having to maintain my prestige among a curious type of human being. The rascals who tenant my home must believe that I am capable of protecting them under all circumstances, collectively and individually. It was not a part of my plan that you remove one of them from the Midnight Club, and I am still puzzled as to how you did it. You must release this man at once."

"And?"

"I will in return release Miss Reith and your agents."

Blord waited. After a moment there was still silence. A faint perspiration moistened his lean face. "Is that all?" he asked finally. "What's the catch?"

"No catch."

Blord said in a blank amazement, "You're going to release some fifty men and women and a spaceship in return for one cheap Jack?"

"One human being—or a million. When there are so many of you, it is difficult to assign value to mere numbers."

Blord's fingers jiggled the eldoplate adjuster, but the darkness of the plate merely shifted unevenly. No visualization came. He remembered something, and said, "I get it. That favor you promised to do for me a few months ago. This is it."

"M-i-s-t-e-r Blord!" There was no anger or reproach in the mechanical tone, but the slurring of sound brought an implication of emotion. "Do you really believe that I would stoop to kidnapping your friends, and then releasing them in order to cancel a promise I made to you?" The voice seemed to grow more metallic. "I am depending entirely upon your unsurpassable sense of logic."

To Blord, it was as obvious as the difference between night and day. The Skal was like *this*. Human measuring sticks didn't apply to it. A fifty-foot lizard that had men murdered and enslaved women was no more criminal than a man who killed or bred lizards. Except that from the human point of view, the thing must be exterminated like some poisonous snake.

"But now," the Skal was rasping, "enough of this. You have until tomorrow noon to make up your mind. Good-by, my admirable friend. You have not been very bright tonight, but I imagine the lady had something to do with that." There was a chuckle, followed by a click as the eldophone shut off.

Chapter 9

The council of war was not going well. Blord sat in the chair before his desk, sunk in gloom. Magrusson, portly, thick-cheeked, newly arrived in response to Blord's urgent summons, occupied the enormous easy-chair to Blord's left. A slim yet powerful young man with cold, thoughtful gray eyes, stood chain smoking, back pressed against the jamb of the door facing Blord. Doc Gregg lounged on the window sill.

From the secretary's chair at Blord's right, Evana said, "But what did the Skal mean about depending on your sense of logic?"

Blord did not answer, nor did anyone else break the silence that slid in hard upon her words. He felt no annoyance at a question that had so obvious an answer. In fact, after his own exhibition of mental aridity while the Skal was talking the night before, it might be a good idea to readjust his entire conception of stupidity. He smiled bleakly, then he noted, pleased, that she seemed not the least put out by the fact that she had been snubbed. It was, he thought, another sign of her amazing growth. She sat slim, chic, self-possessed, and she went on after a moment, coolly:

"If the Skal was foolish enough to release fifty people in exchange for one, that is *its* weakness, not ours. We must simply take the precaution of not entering its strongholds in future, and carry on as if this whole thing hadn't happened. After all, it only acts through men who cannot possibly be as clever as Mr. Blord."

Blord directed a wan grin in her direction. "The brain we're fighting is not human. Frankly, I cannot imagine how to outthink the Skal, who won't believe anything until it has applied its own brand of tensor logic." He groaned. "It's the old story. I swore, when I first came out to the Ridge Stars that I wouldn't try to become a reformer.

"Every day a million major crimes are committed in the Ridge Stars. For an individual to do anything about that is like trying to visit one millionth of the suns in the galaxy during a lifetime. On top of that, Magrusson will tell you that I'm losing ten million or more stellors every day I ignore my own business." He finished in a rush of gloom, "And so—in spite of all this—I get myself mixed up with the undefeatable Skal!"

The plump man was nodding. "Now you're talking sense, Artur. Look, I've brought along a shipload of important documents. It'll take you a month to read them, let alone okay them. How about forgetting this Skal business, and start in on them now?"

Blord said, "What do you think, Cantlin?"

The lean, gray-eyed man shrugged. "I got a shock when you told me what we were up against."

Blord turned to Ellen Reith, who had been silently watching the scene. He said, "And you, Miss Reith?"

She was, he saw, frowning. She glanced up and stared at him with puzzled, appraising eyes. She said slowly, "I'm like Miss Travis. I'd like to know what the Skal meant about your sense of logic."

"It was warning me," Blord's glance took in both women, "not to bother its men again until I had eliminated it. In other words, it challenged me directly, a challenge which it confidently believes I will not dare accept."

Evana, her eyes wide, said: "Oh!" Then: "Of course. I should have realized. But what about?—" She stopped.

Ellen Reith said earnestly, "Mr. Blord, there seems to be no point in your continuing this. We're evidently up against a-a-a-something . . . , who regards our actions as so much childplay."

Blord said in a drab voice, "We're part of the zoo with which he amuses himself." He stared at the floor, then looked up in abrupt decision. He jumped to his feet. "Cantlin!" he said.

The transition from motionlessness to action was so sudden that it startled almost everyone in the room. But the iron-faced Cantlin straightened casually.

Blord spoke swiftly. "Pay all your agents one thousand stellors bonus, and yourself twenty-five thousand. Keep them all in town just in case we've got to defend ourselves. Except for that, forget the Skal and its whole crew."

"Right, Mr. Blord! I'll be seeing you," said Cantlin. He opened the door, sauntered out, and the door closed softly behind him. Blord nodded at Evana, who nodded back; then she followed Cantlin from the room.

There was a moment's silence in the office, then Ellen Reith said, "So that's what all this melodramatic groaning has been about! When did you discover that Cantlin had betrayed you?"

"Huh?" gasped Magrusson. "What's all this?"

Blord flashed him a bleak smile. "The old trouble with ambitious young men who want to set up as operators on their own. Only he, Miss Reith, Miss Travis and I knew in advance that we were going to the Midnight Club. Yesterday, one of the big banks received a deposit of twenty million stellors, under one of Cantlin's pseudonyms that he didn't know I knew about. I hope we fooled him. The Skal made rather valiant efforts to convince me that it is omnipotent. Part of its stock in trade, you know, is the superstitious awe with which it is regarded."

"You mean," Magrusson said, "you're going on with your plans?"

Blord made no reply. He was lifting the receiver of the interoffice phone. Evana's face came onto the plate. She said quickly, "Marian says she's checked every one of your main eldo and local phones connecting to the labs on the planets you named, Mr. Blord. If there were ever tracers on them, it was done with a skill beyond her ability to detect. I would say, however, that, barring supersuperscience, you can now safely load the ether with secret calls."

"Thanks, Evana. And how about that apartment?"

"It's all ready, Mr. Blord," Evana said. "72. Is that okay?"

"Fine," Blord said. "And you'd better get some sleep yourself now. It's pretty late. Good-night." He clicked off, and stood up. "Your apartment is ready, Miss Reith. Mr. Magrusson, I'm sure, will be happy to conduct you to it."

To Magrusson, he said, "Apartment 72. We'll have to try to improve on that tomorrow, but it will do for tonight."

He smiled again at the woman, "Sleep well, Miss Reith."

The look of disappointment on Ellen Reith's face quickly faded. She made a slight move at him over her shoulder as she followed Magrusson out of the room.

One afternoon, more than a week later, the inner door of Evana's office opened. She looked up from her desk to watch two men emerge from Blord's private office. They were carrying a chest. From inside the room a burst of laughter boomed. Laughter so gleeful and open-hearted that Evana found herself smiling in sympathy. The smile faded as the portly figure of Magrusson came out of the inner room.

His face was wreathed in gloom. He closed the door and stood staring mournfully at the girl. Finally, he shook his head and moaned. "He's crazy! If everybody got their just deserts, he'd lose everything he owns. Did you see that chest?" He motioned vaguely at the door through which the men had disappeared. "Documents relating to ninety million stellors' worth of business. And do you know what he's been doing about them this past week?"

Evana Travis held her peace. She knew very well. And it wasn't that she didn't sympathize with the tubby business manager. Magrusson was quivering afresh, as if the picture he had drawn had jogged a whole set of new nerves into motion.

"Nothing! That's what he's been doing. And now he's just scrawled a note authorizing me to handle it routine fashion, without even looking at any of it, mind you. Without knowing what a single sheet is about. I shall," Magrusson said with sudden firmness, "commit suicide if this goes on much longer. But of course, I forgot." He drew back, and looked at her accusingly. "You agree with him, don't you?"

Evana returned his stare with a serene gaze. She said in a clear, cool voice, "The trouble with you is that you don't recognize genius when you see it." Her voice took on a scathing note, "What do a few million stellors matter? He can't possibly spend all the money he's already made."

Magrusson glared at her. "You're like all the rest of the women around here. The great god Blord can do no wrong. When I think of those women physicists over in a dozen labs on as many planets driving themselves and their assistants—do you know that most of them are not even going home to sleep?—it makes me wonder what the universe is coming to."

His plump arm came up in a trembling gesture as he motioned at the door through which he had just come. His voice shook. "Do you know what he's doing in there now?" he asked. "Firing guns! Hundreds of guns! He's torn down one of the walls, built models of a spaceship and of the Skal's castle, and he's alternately firing from one at the other. But of course, you know!"

He stopped, as though to catch his breath, then he rushed on, "You've been here aiding and abetting him in this crazy scheme to destroy the Skal. Miss Travis"—pleadingly—"If you have any regard for Artur, and any influence over him, try to make him change his mind. The Skal has killed some very bright young men in its time. It's merciless. It doesn't even know the meaning of pity. In its curious way, it seems to enjoy playing cat and mouse with the careers of individuals, taking an inhuman joy in leading on its victims, till finally it gleefully pushes them down into a specially prepared abyss."

The vivid word picture struck home. In spite of herself, Evana felt a coldness. She saw that Magrusson had noticed her troubled expression. He gave her a swift, thoughtful look, then pressed on in a more persuasive voice:

"I admit Artur Blord is a fabulously gifted man. I don't suppose his like is born more than once in a century. But this is a wild thing he's doing. Usually, long before this stage of one of his schemes, he has a working plan, something concrete. He admitted to me just now that he's not trying to develop a new weapon. And besides, it's ridiculous. Not even Artur Blord can call radically new energy guns into existence merely by assigning the problem to a bunch of admiring women."

Once more Magrusson paused for breath, then said, "For once he's overreached himself, and it's up to his friends to save him from himself. You're the one he'll listen to. In my opinion, you will be his first permanent secretary. But it's no good being secretary to a dead man, is it?"

"No!" said Evana sweetly.

Magrusson parted his lips to go on, and then the faint smile on her face must have warned him that the single word was an answer, not to his question, but to his entire appeal. His face darkened. He straightened heavily, then raved, "You're like all the rest, that's what you are! You—"

His voice collapsed as the door to Blord's office burst open and Blord came racing out. "Got it!" he shouted. "The lab just phoned in. They've got the method, Evana." He seemed to see Magrusson for the first time. "You still here?" he growled. "Never mind. You're just the man I wanted to see.

51

Find someone whom I can send to the Skal, a man who will deliver a message."

"A message!" Magrusson's voice sounded weak.

"The message is to tell the Skal that I want it to destroy a spaceship that will approach his castle at 008 sidereal hours six days from now, next Saturday. Tell it that *this is the favor* it promised me a few months ago. Got that?"

"Yes, but—"

Evana's voice cut off Magrusson's bewildered mumbling. She cried, "But who's going to be in the ship?"

"I am," said Blord coolly. He went on blandly, "The Skal is going to do me a favor and destroy itself."

Magrusson groaned, and went out waving his hands in the air, mumbling disjointed fragments of words about insanity.

When the door had closed, Blord stared grimly at Evana. "This is not going to be funny," he said. "I think I'd better dictate instructions to be followed in the event that I fail."

Several hours later, the task was completed, and they sat looking at each other. Evana thought, startled: "He's more serious than I have ever seen him."

Blord said, finally, "As for you, my dear—"

"Yes?"

"I'll leave instructions to have you transported to Doridora III, to your sister's."

The girl did not look at him. She said in a low voice: "Thank you."

There was silence. Then, still without looking at him, she said: "I never thought I'd hear myself talking like this—Mr. Blord, but I had a long visit from Ellen Reith the other day."

She hesitated, her color high. Blord looked at her, but said nothing. She continued in a painfully self-conscious voice: "When I first came here, months ago, I was frightened of you—Mr. Delaney told me I had to expect—" She stopped, in confusion, then went on: "I was dreadfully shocked then. But now—isn't it silly?—"

Once more she stopped, abruptly irritated. "Do I have to say everything?" she demanded.

Blord came out of his chair, and stood looking down at her with a faint, quizzical smile on his face. He said at last, "Evana, I don't want you to undertake anything you may later regret."

Evana reached over and took his hands, "I'm really amazed at myself," she said. "But the Ridge Stars make you grow up awfully fast. Talking to Ellen Reith the other day, I suddenly realized that I was waiting in some vague way for you to marry me. And then, I thought how silly that was, a naive little thing like me expecting to encage so free a man."

Artur Blord laughed softly. "Evana, when Delaney and his group picked you that day, they weren't choosing by guess. The man who finally marries you will be a very lucky man."

She sighed, and echoed: "The man who marries me!—well, I suppose that's your answer. But I'll speak to you about it again, Mr. Artur Blord, so don't think that the matter is ended. And don't feel embarrassed for me. I'm trying to grow up, Ridge Star style, and I'll be very annoyed with you if you try to prevent me."

Blord raised her hand, gently. "Good girl!" he said softly.

Chapter 10

Blord began to feel tense as his ship entered the umbra of Delfi I, and approached the Skal's mountain. He was still too far away to make out the darker outlines of that strange and antique building, the Skal Castle. But it wouldn't be long now. The clock on the dimmed instrument board showed seven minutes of eight; and at eight o'clock, the Skal had promised his messenger, it would carry out Blord's request.

A sound very near and behind his chair brought the

thought to an end. Blord jumped, then twisted around. For a moment, he sat very still. Then he said in a flat voice, "You fool! What are you trying to do, get yourself killed?"

A tingue of pink heightened the delicate coloring of Ellen Reith's cheeks. She stood there, biting her lips. Her eyes were very wide open, very blue, and the faintest mist clouded them. She said, "I didn't intend to come out of hiding until—after. But there's a curious mind pressure in the air. I know it's not from inside my head. It's mechanical, like energy waves that have found the wave length of my brain. You told me that the Skal could read minds and—"

Blord interrupted her. "Back!" he said sharply. "Get into the armored bulkhead, quick! I *feel* the Skal."

She sat down in one of the chairs behind him. She was very white, but she shook her head. "You don't understand," she said quietly. "I came aboard because if you were killed, I can't even imagine what I would do." She finished hurriedly, "Now, please pay no more attention to me."

Even if he had wanted to, there wasn't time to reply to that. The ship was reeling to a halt in the very shadow of the dark castle. And something was groping at his mind. Something—a visualization of a long, reptile body—slid into his brain. It was not an unpleasant sensation this time, perhaps because the Skal was in a state of genuine high amusement, almost human in its pattern.

The mind laughed with glee, and the laughter became a thought: "So, Artur Blord, we meet again. Did you really think to fool me?"

Another burst of not unfriendly laughter came, though the meaning of the thought that accompanied the amusement accepted the challenge of his presence. "For the presumption you have shown, Artur Blord, you die tonight. I will see to it that the favor you requested shall be given you in the exact measure that you asked it: The destruction of your ship with all its contents at 008 sidereal hours shall be accomplished, in spite of the police ships that you have persuaded to follow you on the rash promise that you would destroy my home.

But have patience for one moment while I discover in your mind the nature of your plan."

There was silence, and a distinct sense of the fantastic mind pushing at his brain. Finally, Artur Blord began to laugh softly. "You are, I hope," he inquired solicitously, "reading my mind? Exploring the nature of my plan? Devising means to combat it? Or perhaps," he went on, his voice gently sardonic, "you are discovering that my mind is impenetrable. Just a simple little device," he explained modestly, "that one of my ... er ... wives, as Miss Reith would say," he glanced back at her, ironically, "rigged up. A machine that matches the wave length of the brain's nervous energy, and confuses all except the strongest surface thoughts.

"Nothing new about it, mind you. Discovered quite a few thousand years ago, but the inventor at the time said, 'So what!' If you'd ever been in my co-ordination department, Skal, you'd know that it contains all kinds of similarly useless and almost forgotten devices for aiding and abetting the exploits of Artur Blord. But it's time for action. A pity to have to destroy such an ancient structure as your Castle. And I regret I must terminate our interesting conversation. You haven't been very bright tonight, my admirable friend," he taunted. "Is it possible that you, too, are beginning to believe that Artur Blord never makes a public move until he knows that victory is certain?"

The Skal's amusement remained at the same high unnatural level. Blord felt a thrill of pure fright. The Skal laughed: "There's an old human saying: When in doubt, act. So for your special benefit I shall use my weapons without delay, weapons that in the past have destroyed ships like yours in one burst of fire. Surely, Mr. Blord, you do not expect me to believe that you have, in a single fortnight, discovered a super metal or a super energy blaster with which to defeat me. Good-by, my young opponent."

Blord twisted toward the intricate control board. Straight at the scores of silhouetted dark towers that pierced the black of the sky like great swords, he aimed his pointer device. He was still aiming when enormous green flashes surged from every spire of that multi-turreted building of a forgotten race. From stem to stern, his ship flared, like an emerald suddenly subjected to an intolerable light.

Chapter 11

There were myrid lights on Negor, a gem city on the shores of a restless sea. And the brightest among all those jeweled lights was the Midnight Club, with its ninety entrances on the famous Blord Crescent Drive.

Outwardly, all was brilliance. Every gaming room was packed with players, every cocktail lounge had its swarms of well-dressed men and women. But deep inside the massive array of buildings that was the Club, half a hundred masked men gathered in a great dim, ornamented chamber, and sat complacently listening to one of their number.

"As you know," the speaker was saying, "this is the night when the great Artur Blord intended to destroy our patron, the Skal."

A murmur of laughter interrupted him. He waved his hand for silence, and went on, "In view of the fact that one of our—" his tone grew ironic—"more recent members informed the Skal six days ago that Blord himself would be in the ship which, for some reason he wanted the Skal to destroy, and also because it is now long after midnight—"

His voice trailed. His eyes behind their mask slits widened. Doors began opening, and men were surging into the great chamber, men with powerful shining mobile units in their hands. Simultaneously, the large room lit up bright as day. A voice that had in it the hardness of iron said:

"Anybody that so much as moves, dies! Search them!"

The surprise was complete. They remained motionless. In five minutes a stack of hand weapons attested to the thoroughness of the search the newcomers had made. One of them called out now:

"Okay, boss."

Artur Blord, followed by Ellen Reith, entered the room. The odd thing was that, for a moment, she and not Blord was the center of all eyes. She wore a magnificent fur jacket that contrasted vividly with her dark brown hair.

As though aware of her central position in the scene, Ellen Reith moved forward a few steps. She stood there, with a calm, cool smile while her gaze went slowly along the half-circle of masked men.

Watching her, Blord thought in sudden amusement: "She belongs in scenes like this! Even now, she pauses to accept their tribute of admiration."

He pushed the thought away. He said, "Thanks, Cantlin. I'll make it brief." He raised his voice to a grim resonance. "Gentlemen, you have a choice between death and poverty. There are no other alternatives. It's your money or your life, and this time, for your special benefit, I'm abandoning my policy of taking only twenty-five percent of the profits. This time I want an even one hundred percent. Well, perhaps not a hundred. Ninety-eight will do. I have in mind a certain very foolish member of this gathering."

His voice changed, grew mocking. "Come, come, now, my murderous friends, here's your chance to live. Sign over all your earnings, and I'll turn you over to the Fasser government for trial. You can all, in your own minds, estimate the chance there is of a conviction being made against you in a court of law. But the price of that privilege is high, you scum— Everything you own. I have a charming mechanism that makes people tell the truth about such things as secret bank accounts; so there's no escape at all."

"This is an outrage!" It was the man who had been speaking at the moment when the meeting was interrupted by Blord's men. Blord shot him dead. Ellen Reith uttered a gasp, but Blord paid her no attention.

"Come, come," his voice was relentless. "No delay, please. I assure you I have no patience with the bloody hounds who kept the Skal's Castle filled with kidnaped women. Ah, as I thought, the object lesson was helpful. Step right into this room, one by one. No doubt," he went on in his terrible, mocking fashion, "no doubt you can make more money in time. Provided, of course, you escape the long arm of the law— No, fatty, you don't have to go in. I've got special plans for you. This way, please."

The man indicated stepped out of line. His eyes through his mask slits looked glassy. He said nothing, but stood there beside Ellen Reith staring down at the handcuffs that two of Blord's agents snapped decisively on his wrists.

Ellen Reith looked at him in appalled recognition. "Mr. Magrusson!" she gasped. "You!"

The plump man groaned, but didn't answer.

In spite of herself, she found that she was feeling sorry for the man. She said finally, curiously, "But what happened? Just what did you do?"

Magrusson shrugged, and there was an edge of bitterness in his voice as he said, "I wanted to be a king on my own, of course. So, I just took a commission on all those transactions that, despite all my urgings, Blord would never even look at. I made money enough all right; but like most of the men who come out here with a similar craving, I didn't realize that it takes more than money to make a big-time operator. I'm not the type, that's all."

Ellen Reith was still curious. "But how did you get mixed up with the Skal?"

Animation was beginning to return to Magrusson's face, and his voice was firmer when he answered. "They found out what I had been doing, and blackmailed me." He broke off: "What I don't understand is, what is Cantlin doing here? I *know* he sold out to the Skal."

Ellen Reith sighed. That was a case she knew something about, having acted as liaison. It had given her another, sharper look at the way business was done in the Ridge Stars.

She said, "Artur bribed Cantlin to come back into his sercice."

The transaction still startled her, when she thought of it. Never in her plain-speaking life had she been party to so frank a discussion. Cantlin had suggested that she would have to include herself as part of the bribe; and they had argued that aspect alone for over an hour.

Magrusson's voice interrupted her recollections. "What about the Skal Castle? Has Blord really destroyed it?"

Ellen nodded. Magrusson pressed on, puzzled. "But how?"

"That," said Ellen Reith, "is a question I have yet to ask. As far as I could see, we never fired a shot, but suddenly the castle began to crumble like a house of cards. Artur expects the Skal to get away, but we didn't wait to see. The police are in the castle; they've already captured some of the Skal's weapons. The castle is definitely demolished, but how, I don't know."

Later, back at headquarters on Delfi II, Blord looked from one to another of his guests. Magrusson sat silent. Cantlin, handsome as ever, was elaborately nonchalant. It was apparent to Blord that the young man was more concerned about the impression he was making on Ellen Reith than with any fears he may have had about his future.

Blord twisted in his chair to look at that young woman. She was gazing into space with poised deliberation and only the heightened color in her cheeks showed her awareness of the admiration in young Cantlin's eyes.

Blord glanced at Evana, and grinned. Her answering smile showed comprehension and agreement. Satisfied, Blord turned to Magrusson. He said, "Magrusson, I don't believe you'll make the same mistake twice. You're too old and you've been with me too long to become an operator on your own, and you know it." He stood up and crossed to where the older man sat, and dropped his hand to Magrusson's shoulder. "Come on, old man," he said, "there's work to be done! Surely you've got papers waiting for me to sign!"

The plump man lifted his blue eyes and looked at Blord with a frown. "Artur," he said, "damn it, you make me feel

ashamed, and that's proof I'm not the true operator type."
He climbed to his feet and strode out of the room.

Ellen Reith said, "And what are you going to do about
Mr. Cantlin?"

Blord turned and looked at the man with a cool, appraising stare. He said at last, "I've got a tremendous project
starting up on the newly discovered planet, Deg III. I'd like
right now to offer him a seventy-five percent share to run it
for me. It'll need a man who can act. I knew he'd fit the job
when he carried out those executions last night."

"He what?" There was shock in Ellen's voice. Her eyes
flicked to Cantlin's face, then back to Blord.

"You don't think," Blord said grimly, "that we'd let that
gang stay alive, particularly in view of the fact that there was
no real evidence against them. And particularly since the
Skal made a clean getaway."

Ellen Reith was silent. At last she said slowly, "You're
both terrible men. I only began to realize how terrible yesterday. But go on. What happened to the castle."

"The castle—oh, yes. The castle." Blord turned to Evana.
"Tell them what happened to the castle."

Evana had been listening bright-eyed. Now, her laugh
barely missed being a giggle. She said: "Mirrors—that's all.
Just mirrors."

Blord and she laughed in unison, then Blord went on with
genuine enjoyment of his own astuteness: "My wonderful
physicists rigged up energy mirrors for me on an old radio
beam principle. I told all of you that the Skal would be
defeated when it did for me the favor it had promised, and
that's exactly what happened. The mirrors on the ship didn't
last more than seconds in that green blast. But neither did the
castle walls, or the guns behind them when they received the
reflected blow—"

He stopped as a phone in the next room shrilled the
high-pitched squeal of an interstellar call. The sound ended as
Blord came into vision range, changed to an intense blue
flicker that ended in its turn as he lifted the receiver.

"Artur Blord speaking!"

Before he could say more, a mechanical voice chuckled:

"You are even more clever," the Skal said, "than I believed. However, I assure you I hold no grudges. If we meet again, I shall judge my actions by the requirements of the moment. Good-by, my brilliant one, and good luck."

When Blord had given them the gist of the Skal's words, Evana said slowly, "Do you believe that it actually holds no grudge?"

Artur Blord laughed softly. "The important thing is, the Skal's Castle is permanently out of business. And I think we should just leave it at that." His tone became brisk. "And now, Cantlin, your instructions ought to be ready in about two hours. If you'll get in touch with Mr. Magrusson at that time, he'll have the usual contract ready for you and will give you the details of the job. In the meantime," he looked at Ellen Reith with raised eyebrows, "Miss Reith has not yet had a chance to see our beautiful city of Suderea . . ."

Ellen Reith interrupted. "Thank you, Mr. Blord," she said. She glided forward and slipped her arm inside Cantlin's. The young man glanced at Blord, and shook his head, smiling. "She's a hard bargainer," he said from the threshold. Ellen paused, and looked back for a moment. "Good-by, Mr. Blord," she said. "It was fun."

A moment later, the door closed behind them.

Chapter 12

Blord reclined lazily in a chair on the sun deck of the penthouse. Through the slowly moving smoke rings from his cigarette, he watched Evana with appreciative eyes.

She stood on the divingboard, a slight, graceful figure in a bright green bathing suit. She looked across the pool at him and waved. Then with a swift, experienced movement she caught up her long red-gold hair and swept it inside the protective covering of a yellow bathing cap. Once more she waved in his direction, took a little leap and disappeared into the blue-green water.

She emerged in a burst of spray, swam to the steps, climbed out and came toward him. "That's it," she said. "We'd better get started. I'll go aboard, and you can come as soon as your guest arrives."

Blord smiled. "Sure you've got everything straight now?"

Evana paused in drying herself, and enumerated on her fingers. "You drop me off at my sister's on Doridora III. I stay there with her five weeks. Then you pick me up early morning, Doridora time—though why this exact timing, I don't know."

Blord said blandly: "A major deal, my dear. I'll see you."

He headed for the penthouse, and on to the elevators.

The badge said: "Special Agent!"

Standing there in the racing elevator, Nadlin surreptitiously examined the emblem, then grinned in delight. Life was good. Only three years out from Earth, and already he was in a position of power and importance in the Ridge Star patrol.

He felt a brief, contempt for all the lesser creatures of the universe. Let these fellows like Artur Blord make their money. He personally wouldn't exchange his own adventurous job for ten times the wealth he was about to confer on Blord.

The thought ended as Nadlin saw that the other passenger in the elevator, a young man, was watching him with amusement. Nadlin flushed scarlet, in abrupt knowledge that his examination of the badge and his private glee had been observed.

Ears burning, he turned his back. He found himself staring into a mirror inset in a panel. His image in the glass looked embarrassed. After a moment, Nadlin grinned wryly at the reflection. "You fatuous idiot," he thought. "Serves you right."

He expected the other to get off at a lower floor—surely, in a building with two hundred floors—but when the elevator finally slowed and stopped, the young man said in a pleasant voice:

"Hundred and ninetieth floor is as far as this machine goes, Mr. Nadlin. The elevator to the penthouse is just around the corner."

Nadlin faced about blankly. "You know me?"

The young man put out his hand. "My name's Blord. I was downstairs when they told me you wanted to see me, so I thought I'd ride up with you and look you over."

His smile was engaging, but not to Nadlin. Limply, the young policeman took the extended hand, felt his own shaken vigorously, and then released. He had a distinct and awful feeling that he would like to fall through the floor, even if it meant taking the one hundred and ninety floors in reverse and at gravity speed.

"But see here," he babbled finally, "you can't be *the* Artur Blord. Why, he's the biggest operator in the Ridge Stars; and you're no older than I am. You—"

Gulping, Nadlin stopped himself. With an effort, he pulled his mind together, and said quietly:

"Glad to meet you, Mr. Blord." He managed a grimace of a smile. "I hope you will pardon my astonishment. I was sent here by the chief of—"

"We can talk on our way up," Blord cut him off. "This way, please."

The only thing was, *he* didn't stop talking. It was a neat bit of conversation snatching, and the smoothness of it was not lost on Nadlin. As they entered the second elevator, Blord was saying with a casual swiftness:

"When you were announced, I remembered somebody had told me the patrol considered itself indebted to me because of the ... uh ... assistance I rendered in driving the Skal out of the Ridge Stars a year ago. And, of course, they can't afford to be obligated to individuals. So when I remembered on top of that that someone had told me the police were going to blitz into the little known and still wide open and untamed group of stars known as the Eastern Ridge, and that to do this they would require a thousand Galactic-type space-drive units for patrol vessels now being secretly built, I put two and two together. This way, Mr. Nadlin."

Nadlin scarcely heard the admonition. He was aware that the elevator had stopped. Automatically, he followed Blord into the hallway and across to a gleaming doorway. His whole mind was concentrated on Blord's matter-of-fact presentation. The quick, pleasant voice did not pause for an instant.

"—And decided that the police were going to give me the order for the drives and thus discharge their debt to me. Naturally, it wouldn't do at all to leave the police under obligation—"

He paused in the outer office and took a card from the desk. He glanced at it, then went through a second door into a larger office, Nadlin following. The door closed behind them with a bang. And Nadlin was alone with the dynamic young man.

"—So I accept the contract," Blord finished. "What's the time limit on it, Nadlin?"

Nadlin said dully, "I'm supposed to make sure they're delivered in two months. You see—" Suddenly, he realized what he was saying. He gasped to a halt. At last he said, in amazement, "Good heavens, man! Where did you learn all that? That's secret information! Why, if certain people in those eastern stars found out about our intentions, they'd—"

A *brrr* from the desk eldophone ended his outburst. As Blord turned to face the plate, Nadlin drew back. He was relieved that the interruption had occurred. It gave him time to organize himself. The head and shoulders of a plump man appeared on the eldoplate. The very first sentence the man spoke drew Nadlin's fascinated attention.

"Artur, I got hold of Edee Calder about those space drives."

"Yes?" Blord's tone was questioning.

"She won't sell the ore. She warns us to stay away from Yelt VII."

Nadlin couldn't see Blord's face. But the man stiffened visibly. His voice came, abruptly harsh. "So she's still resisting any attempt at Yelt's development."

His tone grew cold. "We'll accept the challenge. As you know, the mining fleet with two thousand armed men is already en route. Have them land. No provocation, mind you. Tell the men to stay at least a hundred miles from Miss Calder's Lake Nem settlement, but to get nine hundred thousand tons of ore. Meanwhile, I'll carry out our original plan of going to see her. That's all for now, Magrusson."

"One minute!" The plump man spoke quickly. "Artur, a point of information: There's something wrong with the Calder woman. She's the worst physical wreck you ever saw. She's a walking corpse, if I ever saw one."

"Okay!" Blord nodded with a curt indifference. He whirled on Nadlin. "If we've only got two months, there's no time to lose. Come this way."

Nadlin followed. His mind was in the throes of trying to grasp what he had just heard. Evidently this man's corporation was already at work on his case. A case that he hadn't even presented yet. With a start, he saw that they had emerged onto a roof garden, and that a spaceship floated there. It was a long, slim, rakish-looking machine with the speed lines of a patrol vessel. The interior was that of a small luxury liner.

"I'll show you your room later," said Blord. "For the moment, grab one of those seats while we take off."

Almost, Nadlin echoed: "Take off!" Just in time he stopped himself and slumped into one of the indicated anti-gravity chairs. He sat there feeling like an atom clinging precariously to the outer rim of a tornado, in desperate danger of being shaken off. The empty feeling faded as the swift minutes passed. The first effects of the spaceship's initial velocity wore off. His mind untangled further, and there was time to observe his surroundings and to study his companion.

Artur Blord's back was to him. He sat in the control chair, intently watching the plates on the instrument board before him. Every few seconds he made minute adjustments on a series of dull black directional dials. Finally, he seemed satisfied. He stood up, and came down from the dais on which the controls were located. Nadlin stared at him curiously, conscious that he was really seeing the man for the first time. Before, everything had been confused; now, he had time to look.

Artur Blord's lean, distinctive countenance, was topped by dark, wavy hair. Its sensitivity was accentuated by the firm chin and mouth. The fine dark eyes smiled at Nadlin as Blord sank into a chair. He held out the card that he had taken from the desk in the outer office. "Read this," he said. "It will give you a clearer picture of my plans. Meanwhile, let me see your contract."

The exchange was made silently. Nadlin examined the card with absorption. It read:

YELT VII

The operator on this sparsely habited planet is E. D. (Edee) Calder. She is the only woman operator I know of; and she has held her position by determined political control of the planet through her money. She is said to be quite youthful—in her middle thirties.

FIRST VALUE: Large deposits of the ore from which crystalline steel for space drives is made, located in hills and mountains all around Lake Nem.

SECOND VALUE: Exploitation should be interesting—if only because of woman operator.

Chapter 13

Nadlin kept his gaze down, nonplussed. In the upper brackets of the police force, such amorality as was suggested by the

PLANETS FOR SALE

reference to the woman, was frowned upon. Three years of
service discipline and morality had stamped that frown on
Nadlin's character. True, his chief had told him that he might
learn a great deal from Blord. And true, also, if the woman
was really a physical wreck she wouldn't be—interesting—
but—

A melodic scream from the control board interrupted the
sharp, disapproving thought. He watched alertly as Blord
climbed the steps and sank into the control chair. The man
spoke swiftly for several minutes in a very low voice. At last
he looked around and beckoned Nadlin. Nadlin mounted
gingerly to the dais. Blord began at once:

"My general manager, Mr. Magrusson, has opened a channel for us through the registered circuit. As you probably
know, the circuit provides an automatic record of contracts
being signed, and is completely secret, never to be seen unless
a court dispute arises. You have no objection to signing?"

For a moment, he hadn't. Under the pressure of that
persuasive voice, he actually reached for the extended pen.
Then he drew back. He thought in exasperation: Wasn't he
ever going to stop being a block of wood in his relations with
this man? He held his voice steady as he said, "Just one or
two questions first, Mr. Blord. I have heard of this debt
which the police owe you; not in detail, but apparently it
does exist. It makes the situation difficult. Should you, for
instance, find yourself unable to deliver the goods within the
specified time, the patrol is most unlikely to be harsh with
you; and at the same time its own plans will be seriously
disrupted.

"I have heard," his voice deepened and he felt surer of his
ground, "that the Ridge Star branch of the Interstellar Drive
Corporation is the only firm capable of manufacturing a
thousand Galactic type drives at short notice. I hope it is
clear to you that it is the special, government galactic drive
that is required under this contract. The drive manufactured
for commercial use by the Ridge Star Company which was
organized after the interplanet competition that was held a
year or so ago is not the one we're interested in. There are,

of course, other firms who manufacture these Galactic drives, but they do so for the high-priced luxury trade only, and their output is small.

"Our idea is that you should be able to make a deal with Interstellar as a subcontractor, thus sharing in the profit. But," he finished, "if it should so happen that you are unable to make such a deal, it would be well to know it before signing this contract."

Nadlin felt better now. He had put the case of the patrol squarely up to this curious young man, and if the registered circuit had been open during his speech, then his objections were not permanently and legally recorded. He saw that Artur Blord was smiling at him.

Blord said, "I have two reasons for believing that Interstellar will accept my contract. The first is that Greg Mearsley, president of Interstellar, is a personal friend of mine. The second is that I am somewhat annoyed at the patrol heads for thinking they owe me something. Accordingly, I am going to pay Interstellar their full retail price for the drives, taking no profit whatsoever for myself."

"Wait!" Blord's voice was clipped and cool. "As you know, crystalline ore for drive steel is rare and difficult to extract. There are firms that retail it in small quantities, but the rule is: if a company wants a space drive, it must locate and mine its own ore. All the main operators, all the big freight and passenger services, have auxiliary mining services. That is where my profit will come in. My main objective actually, is to help the patrol, and to cancel its supposed debt to me."

The eldophone *brred* for attention. It was the plump man. He was perspiring. He puffed, "Important ... Haven't been able to locate Mearsley of Interstellar Drive, Artur, but I've got Crofers, the vice president, on the eldo. He wants to talk to you."

"Eh?" said Blord; and Nadlin instinctively drew closer at the sharpness of his tone, to insure that he would miss nothing.

The plump man said hurriedly, "I'll keep the registered circuit open for you."

His image vanished. In his place flashed the head and shoulders of a thick, saturnine individual. The stranger said softly:

"Ah, Blord!"

The tone of the voice would have been enough. Here was a profound mutual dislike. Blord broke the silence, "Where's Mearsley, Crofers?"

"Oh," Crofers' tone was silk smooth, "he's around. If you can locate him, you're welcome."

"I'll find him. But I gather you're not going to manufacture my drives for me. Why? Refusal is illegal, you know."

"I'll take my chance. Interstellar is not required to sell as a subcontractor."

Blord flashed, "It is, when the full retail price is offered. You haven't a legal leg to stand on."

The other man shrugged. "I don't know just what you're pulling. But I'm not involving Interstellar. When we get an order direct from the real user, as we inevitably must, we'll fill it. You'd better hurry up and turn the contract back to them." He grimaced knowingly. "I hear they've set a two-month time limit. Good-by, Sir."

There was a click. Blord said, "All right, Magrusson, switch in the circuit." He turned to Nadlin, and held out the pen. "Sign please," he said.

"B-but—" said Nadlin wildly.

The dark eyes mocked him. The arm and hand that held out the pen remained firmly extended. Uncertain, confused, conscious that Ridge Star industrial politics was too much for him, Nadlin took the pen. Bending low to hide his misgivings, he signed.

It was on the third day out that Nadlin awakened to realize that the ship had come to a stop. He emerged from his room in time to see Blord carrying a bag toward the airlock. Behind Blord there walked a red-headed young woman of startling beauty.

She disappeared into a lifeboat. Blord came back presently; the airlocks closed with a soft thud; there was a pause; and then the yacht began to move again.

Blord turned from the control board, and said: "My secretary is visiting her sister on Doridora III."

Nadlin said nothing, but just for a moment his policeman's heart thawed to admit the wish that someday he might have a secretary who looked like that.

The seven days that followed added nothing to Nadlin's knowledge. He had expected to at least become better acquainted with Artur Blord—but the man seemed almost to have forgotten him. He spent his time either sitting at the eldophone talking to members of his far-flung organization, or in signing great stacks of papers. If he really slept, Nadlin was not aware of it. True, the man took frequent catnaps of from twenty to thirty minutes duration, but never once in the days they spent on the ship, did Nadlin see him actually go to bed for a night's sleep.

Watching him and his apparently unlimited capacity for work, Nadlin thought, startled: Those stories he had heard about this man's exploits! Could they possibly be true? The idea was revivifying. But he wished that Blord would be less taciturn about his search for Mearsley, the president of Interstellar. What did the man expect him to think under such circumstances but that the president of Interstellar was still among the missing? He was still worrying about it on the eighth morning when the blue sun of Yelt sprang out of the great dark. A blazing glory of fire, it grew bigger and brighter, ever brighter, pouring its ravenous energy through the length and breadth of its twenty-four planet system.

It was high noon below as their ship sagged, still at full deceleration, through the thick mist that was the upper atmosphere of Yelt VII. There was the usual sense of awful and unearthly speed as they leveled off above a land of virgin forests and mountains. They flashed over a great valley where a dozen of Blord's mining ships sprawled, disgorging machinery. Moments later, the lake of Nem appeared on the horizon, and it was only seconds after that that they came to a full stop over a scraggly settlement.

Standing beside Blord, Nadlin stared through the bottom

vision-plate at the town of Lake Nem. There seemed to be about five buildings of importance, and they were all located somewhat outside the actual town. One of the structures was a great white mansion standing on the shore of the lake. The other four buildings were clustered a few hundred yards back from the water, long, low, squat affairs, typical primitive factories.

"It doesn't look," said Nadlin, "as if she's ever been able to get many immigrants." He jumped as a puff of gray fire leaped from the doorway of one of the buildings. Beneath his feet, the floor quivered. Nadlin dived for the nearest antigravity chair. He made it, as the ship rose like a rocket into the enveloping mists that eternally blanketed the seventh planet of the hot Yelt sun.

Nadlin made his way back to the dais. "Yow!" he said. "She means business." He was about to go on, when he saw that Blord was smiling at him. It was a companionable smile, but it brought Nadlin back to reality. His excitement vanished. He was suddenly not so sure that he had enjoyed the brief danger. It was all very well to take risks in the course of patrol duty; but he was a police executive now, with a mission. It would be silly to get himself killed in one of these inter-operator wars.

The eldophone clamored an angry interruption to his thoughts. A woman's face came onto the plate. The sight of her startled Nadlin. He knew instantly that it must be Edee Calder. No other human face could possibly fit the description that Magrusson had given of her on the first day.

Her eyes were black, sunken pools. Her face was the color of snow, drawn and horrible. Her mouth was a twisted, colorless line. Yet strangely she didn't look old. There were few lines even on her forehead, and when she spoke, her voice though weak and a little harsh was that of a young woman. Here Nadlin thought, was a pretty woman in the final stages of a virulent wasting disease. She said coldly, "Artur Blord, I presume?"

"Correct. Madam, I would like to convince you that you are being unwise in—"

She cut him off: "I have decided to let you continue your mining operations where your ships have landed provided—"

"Eh!" said Blord sharply. "Then why the gunfire? And why the earlier refus—"

"Provided," the wan voice went on with a semblance of firmness, "neither you nor your men make any attempt to come within a hundred miles of my settlement here, and provided you pay me half a stellor a ton for the ore you take. If that agreement is broken in any way, the charge per ton goes up to one stellor. Is that clear?"

"Now," said Blord heartily. "Now, you're talking."

"Very well. I have taken our conversation on a wire. The contract will be drawn up, and sent you; and we can sign later on the registered circuit. That is all."

The eldoplate went dark. The two men stared at each other. During the conversation, Blord had shown no sign that he was affected, but now Nadlin saw that the man was jarred out of his basic calm. Blord gasped:

"Did you see *that?*" He added in a frowning afterthought, "I wonder what she's hiding."

Nadlin scarcely heard the last sentence. He said in a blank horror: "She looks as if leeches—disease-ridden leeches—have been drinking her blood."

"Leeches!" said Blord. He sounded startled. But the emotion behind the sound must have been more violent than the expression of it, for he jumped to his feet and his eyes were wide with calculation. With an effort he seemed to control himself. He stood tense, and he muttered: "But why would they . . . what . . . it could be!"

He looked at Nadlin in a fever of excitement. "You've hit it, man! Somehow, in spite of all precautions, one or more of those *things* escaped." He broke off. His face became a mask of anger. "Nadlin," he said, "you and I are going down there tonight, and if some of those *things* are there, we'll come back tomorrow prepared to do a little plain and fancy exterminating. That is," he smiled grimly, "if they, with their superfast senses, don't get us first."

It was like listening to a strange language. Nadlin said

anxiously, "But what about Interstellar Drive? After all, it will take a month at least for the drives to be manufactured. And besides, I'd like to report personally to my superiors."

There was no reply. His eyes narrowed, Blord pushed past him, and the door to his cabin banged shut.

Later that day, Nadlin saw him at the eldophone, talking rapidly, then listening to what seemed like a monologue from the other end. Watching the scene, Nadlin knew once more the emotion that, it seemed to him, was fast becoming normal in his relationship with Artur Blord; the helpless conviction that he was beyond his depth and moving ever deeper into darker waters.

Chapter 14

In the gathering dusk, Nadlin crouched with Blord beside a trail. A soft breeze, rich with the tang of warm lake water, brushed his cheeks. And every minute he felt more like a fool. It was hard to believe that he was lying here on a damp, marshy embankment, embroiled in a senseless venture, knowing that every hour spent thus endangered more the enterprise for which he was responsible. It might even have been different if Blord had been a little freer with facts.

Nadlin groaned inwardly and gave himself up to his environment. After all, he was here. Whatever happened involved him just as if he had come willingly. In the near distance, he could make out the first and biggest of the four factories that had been visible from the air. The building was a slate gray in color, half hidden by trees. From its interior came the hum and clamor of machines. Farther away, but to the right, gleaming white in the half darkness, was the Calder woman's imposing house which he had also seen sketchily from the air. A weary side glance showed Nadlin that Blord was studying the distant veranda through field glasses. He must have sensed Nadlin's gaze, for he turned and said in a low voice:

"This looks to me like the trail between the house and the foundry. We'll stay right here for a while. I have an idea your "leeches" will keep a pretty close tab on everything that's doing."

It was the words that did it, the reference once more to something that Blord had not yet troubled to explain. Nadlin cut him off with a cold fury that, in one jump took him past the hurdle of the necessity of being polite to this tremendously important young man. He said: "For days you've been evading every question I've asked, grinning at me whenever I was persistent. And now you've dragged me out here on a wild chase. I was warned you had a habit of running off on tangent schemes. But I surely never thought, when I got into this business, that I'd be lying in a ditch with a madman who babbles of leeches and ignores vital contracts that he's signed."

A joyous laugh interrupted his tirade. Nadlin shivered with anger, and parted his lips for a second outburst. Before he could speak, Blord said, "I've been waiting for you to blow up."

Nadlin said nothing.

The other chuckled. "If there's one thing I can't stand for long, it's a man who remains on his manners. You can't talk to people like that. They won't open up. Now, listen, Jimmy . . . that's your name, isn't it—"

Before Nadlin could more than grasp that the lecture was over, before he could begin to decide how to take this new development, Blord was rushing on. "I didn't tell you anything because you're a policeman; and, if you knew the truth, or what I suspect to be the truth, your first act would be, figuratively of course, to blow your police whistle and bring a lot of other policemen onto the scene. Frankly," he went on coolly, "I'm not accustomed to having the law puffing and heaving at my side. And I wouldn't *think* of putting them under further obligation to me."

He paused; then said slowly, "Have you ever heard of the human mutation called a zilth?"

"Zilth!" Nadlin echoed the word. He gasped.

Blord said softly, "That's right. You've got it."

Nadlin hardly heard. His mind was a whirlpool as he reviewed what he knew about those curious human creatures, the zilths. Zilths were descendants of the first human beings to come to one of the Ridge Stars. Their ship had crash-landed on one of the planets of the Zilth sun, thus cutting them off from all communication with the outside world. For nearly two hundred years they had lived in isolation.

And they had changed. Changed under the grip of an unimaginably malignant disease. Nine tenths of the original settlers died raving lunatics. The survivors and their descendants suffered a violent metabolistic and cerebral transformation. In all the universe of man, nothing like it had ever been seen before. The change involved an enormous speed-up of reflexes; faster acting muscles; swifter mind response. It was a genuine physical and mental mutation of the first order. There was only one thing wrong with it: every zilth remained a carrier of the disease that had made him what he was.

The commission of doctors who, with an array of battleships behind them, investigated, recommended that the entire Zilth planet be "fenced" off. And that this be enforced by the most rigid system of police control conceivable. Outside this area zilths were to be shot on sight; and inside it there was to be a scientifically planned decreasing birth control designed eventually to wipe out the race. Laws were accordingly passed. No zilth, so far as he knew, had ever escaped. But if they had—were he and this madman Blord actually seeking contact with them? He mumbled words of protest. And was cut off.

"Ssssh!" Blord hissed. "Here comes somebody. Don't forget the senses of zilths react five to ten times as fast as those of normal human beings. And since this is only a preliminary investigation, I haven't taken any of the usual safety precautions."

Through the tall, gently swaying grass, Nadlin made out two shadowy shapes approaching rapidly along the pathway. They were extremely elongated, extremely thin. Chilled, he found himself remembering a picture he had seen of zilths, throats starting at the chin like puffed-up frogs, eyes protruding, bodies unnaturally attenuated—unnaturally long. The thought flamed: His badge! If they were caught and—"

He made the mistake then, of reacting to that sudden thought, of shifting his position and moving his arm, as he brought his badge from under the lapel of his coat and down to the skillfully concealed pocket in the seat of his trousers. . . .

Chapter 15

The blackness receded from Nadlin's vision. He was, he found, lying with his hands bound behind his back and on a metal floor in the control room of what seemed to be a junked spaceship. The room was bare metal, no ornamentation, no visible automatic machinery and devices. The drab, stripped effect extended to the limits of his narrow range of vision. A movement glimpsed from the corner of his eye ended the thought. He twisted about. And stiffened. Artur Blord lay ten feet away, watching him. Shining strands of wire held his legs together, and his hands were awkwardly behind his back.

"They're away right now," Blord said, "but according to my timing, they ought to be back any minute."

The information brought no easement. Nadlin was thinking: This was *his* fault. It was he who, back there on the trail, had moved after being warned not to, and instantly the two zilths had darted at them. There had been a sledgehammer blow, he recalled.

With a start, he remembered what the action of his was that had caused their discovery. His badge, with its special functions, was saved. He felt better. But it would be folly to use the badge to release Blord and himself if, just as they were climbing to their feet, the zilths broke in on them. And yet, to wait for the arrival of these horrible disease carriers! Sweat broke out on his face.

He began to work his hands downwards toward the secret pocket. The first slash of pain stabbed from the wrists up either arm and lodged like a drilling needle high up in the shoulders. The agony was as concentrated as the flame of a blaster. It stopped him. The process would have to be much slower. Waiting for the anguish to subside, he said, "What I can't understand is: how come there's no record of any zilth ever getting away from his planetary system?"

Blord was smiling grimly, "But there is. I checked on that the afternoon of the day we were captured. The escape was pulled off about twelve years ago by two zilths named Wilf Peterson and Hidlo Creighton, crew members of one of the slow interplanetary ships permitted zilths. At the time they radioed they had crashed on a meteor, and were never heard from again. Actually, their ship was not wrecked. Somehow, it had been equipped with a makeshift interstellar drive. And here it is."

"Huh!" said Nadlin.

He looked around him. And he saw as with new eyes. All the incompleteness, the old-fashionedness was explained. He had seen pictures of ships like this in his textbooks. Blord was speaking again:

"I suppose they headed for Yelt because it's the nearest sun but one to Zilth. The trip with their makeshift drive took them nine years. I figured that out on a basis of some translations of medical books I have in the library of my ship. According to them, the condition in which we saw Edee Calder is in the stage reached at the end of the third year—"

77

He stopped. He lay, the muscles of his face contorting. He said finally with a strange quietness, "I'd almost forgotten her. Her whole settlement must be infected."

There was silence. Nadlin had time to remember a thought that had been quivering at the back of his mind since the first moment of his return to consciousness. He said uneasily, "Why have they left us alive?"

Blord laughed harshly. "They've caught a policeman and the owner of the fleet of freighters they tried so hard, through Edee Calder, to prevent from landing. In their place, wouldn't you try to figure out some way of using us?"

"I think," said Nadlin slowly, "we'd better get out of here. I've got a police method of escape that—" His words trickled to a halt, because Blord was shaking his head, regretfully. Nadlin twisted at his wrists, tensed himself against the anguish, and reached for the hiding place of the badge. The pain flashed in livid strength. He reached the tiny pocket.

As he slowly withdrew his fingers from the emptiness they found, he heard Blord say, "I'm afraid they searched us rather thoroughly."

The clangor of a distant air lock jangled across the words. Almost instantly there came the muffled sound of voices. The zilths had returned.

Nadlin's tensed muscles relaxed. After a minute the sounds were not only as far away as ever, but growing more confused. Puzzled, he glanced at Blord, whispered, "What are they doing?"

Blord shrugged. And when he spoke it wasn't in answer to Nadlin's question. "Look, Jimmy, don't you worry too much. We're going to get out of this somehow. I have great faith in my luck, and in certain skills I have. Just don't be too surprised at anything I do."

Nadlin suppressed the impulse to point out that luck has usually been derived from an intricate combination of positive capacities and abilities, among which foresight stood first. He suppressed the thought because, no matter how basically innocent he was of having caused their present predicament, his *was* the immediate responsibility for their capture. He said finally, "This confidence of yours—may I ask some questions?"

"Go ahead."

Nadlin began quietly: "The first question will sound quite silly perhaps but—has Mearsley been found yet?"

Blord looked at him. "Not up to the time of our capture." He added, "And it's just as well, too, considering everything."

Nadlin ignored the postscript. "Have you any idea how long we've been here?"

"Seventeen days."

"WHAT?" In spite of all his will, Nadlin was torn completely out of his calmness. He thought in a pure mental anguish: *Seventeen days.* Seventeen days added to the eleven it had taken to get to Yelt left little more than a month in which to discharge his duty to the patrol. A month of that would be needed for the manufacturing, which wouldn't begin until Blord signed the contract with Interstellar. Groaning inwardly, he discontinued that painful trend of thought. He said hopelessly, "How do you know?"

"The fellow," said Blord, "who tackled me got my gun before I could fire, but after that he had quite a fight. I realized the game was up, however, when the other one joined him, and so I bit hard into my one false tooth, releasing a little of the many-purposed chemical inside. By using just a small amount of it each time, it effectively counteracted the sleeping potion they've kept giving us. They finally stopped giving it to me." He finished simply, "Since then I've been lying here waiting for you to come to."

A picture formed in Nadlin's mind. He saw the fight as it must have been, himself instantly demobilized, Blord reacting with an almost zilthlike ferocity and almost getting away. It was not a satisfying picture. Particularly the part played by the police left much to be desired. After a moment, he said, "But what about food? Surely in seventeen days we—"

Blord said, "You've been fed intravenously. You'll probably find yourself pretty weak when you try to stand up. They—" He broke off hurriedly: "You'd better ask your questions. Each time they've come in the past, they've first loaded equipment aboard, and then marched in here."

Nadlin shook his head wearily. "Nothing more to ask. What I had in mind is answered by the fact that seventeen days have passed. You see," he shrugged, "I was hoping that you had made some advance protective preparations. But I have an idea that anything like that would have functioned before the end of seventeen days."

Blord nodded reluctantly. "Even if Macklin, my chief mining engineer, did start a search, he couldn't possibly find us because this ship is buried under a cliff on the opposite side of the planet from Lake Nem. So—"

He did not finish the sentence. Even if he had, Nadlin wouldn't have heard. His gaze had flicked toward the open door that led to the adjoining section of the ship. There was the sound of shuffling footsteps.

Chapter 16

The zilths came in, smiling. And in the full glow of the ceiling lights, they looked considerably less alien than he had expected. The smile somehow deflated their froglike throats, and seemed also to set in operation muscles that drew their eyes deeper into the eye sockets. For a bare moment, they looked human and except for an unnatural suggestion of plainness, normal. And then, their smiles faded. It was as if in a flashing instant they had put on demon masks—or *taken off* human ones. Elongated, nightmarish things, they bent for a moment beside Blord, examining his bonds, and then they came over to Nadlin. He shrank. But they seemed not to notice. And all that happened was that hard fingers touched his wrists. Then they were in his line of vision again, standing talking in low tones.

Finally, one of them walked over and began to unwind the wires from Blord's wrists and ankles. The long strands came clear. "Get up!" the zilth commanded curtly.

Blord staggered to his feet, but fell instantly. He lay there grimacing with pain. At last he smiled up at his captors. "I've got poor circulation anyway," he said, "and you didn't help any with those wires."

The zilths stood impassive, Nadlin had time to estimate that they were easily six feet six inches tall. After about five minutes of rubbing his wrists and ankles Blord stood up. "Okay," he said. "What now?"

There was silence, then: "You are still prepared to send those mining ships away?"

The use of the word "still" made Nadlin blink. He thought: Had Blord discussed the matter with these *things* before? He waited, chilled by suspicion. He listened incredulously as Blord said:

"I told you I would, didn't I? But first I want you to repeat your promise to me for the benefit of my friend here."

The zilth faced Nadlin impatiently, its lips twisted in a sneer. "Your friend was clever enough to recognize that he was caught and agreed to co-operate. We promised to release both of you as soon as we had made good our escape. I hope that you will yield yourself to the spirit of that co-operation."

Blord must have caught the expression on Nadlin's face. He said brusquely, "Don't be a fool, man. The important thing now is that we save our lives."

"You fantastic idiot!" Nadlin shouted. His voice failed him. He lay there, appalled, then found his voice again: "You madman! Can't you see that they intend to kill us the moment we've served their purpose? Why, they're not even pretending very hard. They—"

He saw with a sickening sense of failure that he was making no impression. He lay there then so angry that his eyes blurred, his mouth grew dry, and felt too awkward for speech.

Blord stared at him curiously, and said finally, "Why should they kill us? As soon as they leave here, they can vanish into a night so vast that it will take a man at least three hundred million years to explore thoroughly his own little dust mote of a galaxy let alone the others beyond." He added, almost as an afterthought, "As evidence of my own complete faith in the logic of what I've just said, I told them where my spaceship was hidden."

"You what?"

It seemed to Nadlin that his life had become a succession of melodramatic shouts. Blord seemed not to have heard this one. He was turning to the zilths. He said, "Don't worry about my friend. He just woke up. I'll guarantee to bring him around before you come back here again."

The zilth who had not spoken before said coldly, "There is no next. We are leaving as soon as your mining ships have gone. You will remain on this ship with Wilf. Your friend will come with me aboard your former machine. And if we should be challenged, and he refuses to front for me on the eldoplate, I shall eliminate him."

Nadlin saw that Blord was hesitating, frowning, but he said finally, urgently, "I'm sure my friend won't be such a fool. He knows as well as I that there are torture methods that can make human beings do anything. So why not recognize in advance the futility of obstinacy. Hear that, Nadlin?"

Nadlin turned his back. It seemed to him that he had never in all his life so thoroughly despised a man. So this was the famous Artur Blord, the man whose courage and audacity was a byword, the great operator who always outsmarted his enemies, the financial and industrial wizard who never failed to deliver the goods. What a laugh! What a monstrous and unprincipled propaganda must lie behind that false reputation. Abruptly, he realized that Blord was at the eldophone, and one of the zilths was saying:

"If you attempt betrayal, we'll cut you off before you can finish the first word."

Blord said, "Don't worry about me. I'm only too aware of the speed of your reactions." There was a pause, then, "Oh, hello, Macklin ... Now don't get excited. Sure, I'm all right. They've found Mearsley? Well, it's too bad. Tell him from me he's out of luck, and that he can blame Crofers for the loss of the biggest contract they'll have this year.

"But now listen: I want you to pull up stakes and go to that job on Carox A II. You know the set-up. And get busy. I want you out of Yelt in two days. I'll be seeing you. So long." There was a click.

The door opened. Nadlin looked up from the bed on which he had been tossed so many hours before. "Oh," he said, "it's you."

The zilth was bleak. "A ship has appeared in the distance. I think it is my companion but you can see yourself that it would be foolish for me to put my image on the eldoplate. You will accordingly prepare yourself to front for me."

Nadlin's pulses were leaping. "Ship!" he said. His high hope faded as he saw the expression on the zilth's face. Before the threat that glared down at him, his own eyes narrowed. "You'll get nothing out of me," he said harshly. "I'll die before I make a single move that will keep a thing like you alive to spread disease. Have you no sense of horror at what you're doing? Don't you realize that you can wipe out the human race?"

He stopped. The unnatural, the inhuman ferocity of the creature that was watching him so intently penetrated then. The zilth straightened its features finally, and said in a strangely gentle tone:

"I expected preliminary persuasion would be necessary, so I brought along some primitive equipment that I managed to tinker together in the machine room." It reached into its pocket and produced a thumbscrew. It sat down on the bed beside Nadlin. It was smiling now, and it looked almost human. "But of course," it went on in that same gentle tone, "we zilths are accustomed to working with primitive tools. We, the greatest race in the universe, the superman mutation, the man *after* man, the—"

Its voice rose sharply. It must have noticed the developing

emotionalism, for with a click of its tongue it cut off the words, and sat there smiling. It said softly, "You will pardon my intensity. After all, there is some justification for our— irritation—with man's plans for us. Fortunately—" The smile faded. The protruding eyes glinted. The naked, hideous rage that was almost consuming it stood out like whipcords on its pale countenance. "Fortunately," it said, "we shall some day be in a position to repay every insult, every vile intent, and above all, the insufferable presumption that a higher race must be sacrificed in order to save a lower.

"We shall go, into the great dark, to distant and unfindable planets, and there we shall breed in ever vaster numbers. But we shall come back. Yes, back to conquer and destroy, to raze and avenge, and to rule until *our* special death snatches the weak and makes fellow zilths of the strong."

Once more it clicked its voice into silence with a lingual sound. Then it said, "Let me have your thumb, my friend."

It stopped, and whirled, and snatched at its gun, all in one synchronized action. There was a flash of fire from the door.

Artur Blord pulled the dead body from where it had collapsed on top of Nadlin, lowered it to the floor; and then picked up the thumbscrew and examined it curiously. "I'm glad," he said, "that he was holding this. It interfered with the fastest draw I've ever seen."

He tossed the device onto a table, and pulled a small object from his pocket. In a blank amazement, Nadlin found himself staring at his own police badge. As its dissolving force cut the wires that bound him, he found his voice:

"But—" he gasped wildly, "but . . . but—"

Chapter 17

"It's a good thing," the chief of the patrol police was saying heartily, "for a young man to have an adventure with Artur Blord. The man is an education in himself."

Nadlin nodded gloomily. He was, he realized, being let off easily for failing in his assignment. For five days, ever since he had been transferred from Blord's ship to the patrol vessel that had contacted them late on the sidereal day of his rescue, and brought him to patrol headquarters on Marmora II, he had dreaded this moment of personal report. So far, he had yet to get a word in edgewise.

"Blord has an idea," the chief chuckled, "that young men don't like him. All nonsense, of course. How can anybody help but admire the way he mentioned Carox A II when he was talking to Macklin, his chief mining engineer, with the zilths right there."

Nadlin jumped. He was suddenly acutely conscious of how unperceptive he had been not to see *that* part before. He said involuntarily, "That's the planet that's all ocean except for one tiny island!"

"Exactly." The gray-haired officer was smug. "You don't send mining ships there. It was a long-standing danger signal between Blord and his chief executives, partially nullified by the swift departure of the zilths, but nevertheless an example of his varied technique—as are the multiple devices he has for recapturing his private yacht. Truly, a co-ordinated human being."

"How many men in his place," his superior glowed on, "with the means of escape—your badge—always to hand, would have lain there seventeen days waiting for the zilths to load up from their caches? Caches which it is doubtful we shall find until the planet is thickly settled—even yielding up his own ship, so they would bring more units out of hiding.

"Of course, he didn't have the worry that less well-informed men might have had; of catching the disease. As most intelligent people know, it takes about six months before it becomes communicable, regardless of the intimacy of the relationship with the carrier." The man looked at Nadlin sharply, "You knew that of course, didn't you?"

Nadlin, who had only found out that fact five days ago, mumbled something.

The other continued, "The rest, of course, was logically simple. Zilths require a great deal of sleep, and they die most easily when caught by surprise. When I was having lunch with Mr. Blord an hour ago—"

Nadlin sat up. "Is Blord here?"

"Oh, didn't I tell you? He arrived this morning with the two cargoes." His voice went on, but Nadlin was thinking wryly: The gall of the man, coming here to patrol headquarters like a conquering hero, brazenly ignoring the fact that he had failed his contract. So that was how reputations were sustained. It was an education all right.

The chief's voice crept back into his hearing, "Naturally, we've giving out no publicity until the devil's plot is completely foiled. Even interplanetary travel will be forbidden zilths in future, their primitive ships taken away. To think that these two creatures actually supervised the building of twelve hundred interstellar drives on Yelt in three years, enough to enable half the zilth race to escape. I shudder—"

"Twelve—hundred—drives!" said Nadlin faintly. He saw that the other was rubbing hard hands together in a profound satisfaction.

"Amazing total, isn't it?" the chief said gleefully. "We'll be able to go into the Eastern Ridge a month ahead of schedule. Blord is taking twenty-five percent of the total price, leaving the rest to Edee Calder. Doctors got to her and her workers in time, though it will take about five years to effect a complete cure.

"The trouble is, the patrol will never be able to repay Blord now." He sighed, finished, "So I don't think we'll even try."

Chapter 18

Artur Blord wasn't quite sure just what he was supposed to do, so he wiggled the tumbler, conscious of the intent stare from the two women standing beside his desk. The dark-brown liquid in the glass swished from side to side like so much water. But no water had ever weighed as heavily as that. He dipped his finger into it. It felt cool. Room temperature, he judged. He looked up.

"What can it do, Marian?"

He watched while the pretty woman physicist took an eye dropper from her bag, filled it with the liquid, and squeezed one drop onto an ornamental metal paper weight on the desk. There was a hiss, violent and menacing. The weight began to dissolve. It shook like jelly and then ran into a watery pool that covered half the desk. The woman said, "It will resolidify in about an hour, leaving no trace of the solvent. That drop would have liquefied about a cubic foot of any metal."

Blord frowned thoughtfully. "That means that a few pounds would dissolve objects as large as ships."

"We thought," interjected Evana triumphantly, "that you'd get the idea."

"Where did you obtain it?" asked Blord.

It was the woman physicist who replied. "A routine bribe purchase through one of our contacts in Earth Government Science. I thought I'd show it to you, so you could—" she smiled—"coordinate it."

Artur Blord stared unhappily down at the substance. "Science is getting too far ahead of Society again," he said, and his tone was uneasy. "What's the production problem?"

Her answer was not encouraging. "We could do it," she said, "on less than a billion stellors, which means any big operator could be in full production in about a year."

Blord shrugged. "Well, I suppose there's no use getting upset. Here it is, and we'll have to deal with it."

Marian said, "Well, I wish you luck when you come up against it." She was gathering up her belongings from the desk as she spoke.

A moment later, the door closed gently behind her.

For years, ever since his personal plans had matured, Executive Professor Brian Emerson had waited for an outstanding discovery to be made in one of the many laboratories of which he was head. A discovery that, added to all the others he had stolen from Earth Government Science, would give him the special advantage he felt his purpose needed.

The liquid metal R was it.

He did not flinch from the necessities. There were records to destroy, death to mete out to men who knew about the metal, the experimental spaceship, *Creative Physics*, to be secretly readied, and his own tracks to be covered. Out in space, heading toward the Ridge Stars, the professor examined his position and found it good. He had aboard all the liquid metal R there was in the universe. And of the seventeen men he had decided would be willing to embark on such a venture, only one had had to be killed for refusing.

"Our first task," he said to Hounsley, his chief assistant, when they were five days from their destination, "will be to acquire operating capital. To that end we shall seize the treasure ship, *Tantalus*, which is due to leave for Earth in about two weeks on its next monthly trip. The *Tantalus* will be heavily escorted, of course. But we shall arrive invisible and fire only as many shots as there are ships. There will be no survivors."

There weren't. But afterward Hounsley came uneasily to

the professor. "Sir," he said, "I didn't know you were going to use liquid R to dissolve those ships. I didn't even know we had any aboard."

Professor Emerson had an instinct for trouble. "What's wrong?" he said sharply.

"That liquid metal! You know I was one of the first to learn about it."

"So?"

"I sold a gallon of it to the science department of the Artur Blord Holding Company."

The professor said nothing, only his heavy face, with its incongruous domed forehead, reddened slightly. His blue eyes hardened to the texture of cold steel. When he spoke, his gentle voice belied his fury. "So you were one of the leaks in EGS. It would be easy, of course, to get information where you were in Communications." He paused, "So you sold it to Artur Blord. The great Artur Blord. The man who never loses, who uses even the mightiest operators of the Ridge Stars for his own purposes. I always intended to challenge Blord. Apparently, it's going to be sooner than I would have preferred."

He went on, frowning, "Our problem is that we must first establish ourselves in a safe hideout. Nothing is so important as that. Afterwards, if I know anything about Ridge Star psychology, we'll still have time to head Blord off. The big operators handle their own affairs. They don't go to the police for help."

The thought made him more cheerful.

Evana laid the news item on Blord's desk. Blord, busy reading documents said without looking up: "What does it say?"

"It's about a group of scientists who were killed when the Earth Government Science spaceship, *Creative Physics,* was stolen recently. Professor Hounsley was one of the two dozen dead."

"Hounsley?" Blord said, questioningly.

PLANETS FOR SALE

Evana nodded. "Marian tells me he's the one that sold us the liquid metal she showed you a month ago."

Blord laid down the paper he was holding. "What was the state of the body?" His eyes narrowed slightly.

"It says here—badly damaged, and almost unrecognizable."

"Hmmm! Who else was killed?"

"We have only two of the names on file," said Evana. "Ashleyton—he's listed as an instrument expert, and the head of Earth Government Science—"

"Brian Emerson!—" said Blord, in a startled voice.

And then he was silent. Emerson—the most famous name in science, the man who for the past ten years had been executive professor of EGS.

He stood up. "I think we should get further data on this—the exact condition of the dead bodies, and so on. Meanwhile—knowing Emerson—let's assume he's not dead, and let's assume that by this time Hounsley has admitted he sold us the sample."

He was pacing the floor, thinking out loud. "Emerson will strike at me the moment he gets organized in some safe hideout. We've got to find the hideout and get in the first blow."

He turned toward the desk eldophone. As his fingers reached for the control, a light showed, and the plump facial image of Magrusson appeared on the vision plate. The general manager of the Artur Blord Holding Company, Limited, moaned, "Artur, Philips has been at it again."

"Don't bother me with that stuff now," Blord said hastily. "Listen! Get our agents out in force. I want to know if anything unusual has been happening at any of the known criminal hideouts in the Ridge Stars." He explained briefly what Evana had just told him.

Magrusson seemed not to have heard. "It happened over on Zand III," he said mournfully. "Philips went to Morgan and Dand, and the deal he made with them will cost you ten million stellors during the next year if we confirm it."

Blord relaxed slowly. There was a pained expression on his

90

face as he said, "Well, you'd better confirm it. But try to negotiate some sense into it. And get that information. I want it." He clicked off the eldophone and looked somberly at the woman.

"Philips?" Evana said, "Is that the man who—"

"That's the one," nodded Blord. "As if I haven't got enough trouble. I have to confess I don't know what to do about Philips. I don't dare issue a general warning because it might encourage others to try impersonating me, also. And the local police commissioner here on Delfi II, an old enemy of mine, has actually told me that if anything happens to Philips, he'll issue a charge against me. Even if the police were friendly, it would be hard to prove anything against the fellow. He's beaten a dozen murder-theft charges since he came to the Ridge Stars. He's trying to blackmail me for five million a year."

"If I were you," said Evana, "I'd concentrate on Emerson. Marian says she's scared. These men are SCIENTISTS, in capital letters." She hesitated. "I know this is heresy, but why not go to the space patrol?" She saw the look on his face, and said hastily, "All right, all right. I know the Ridge Star operators don't go to the police with their problems. I'm sorry I mentioned anything so reasonable."

Blord said tonelessly, "You're quite wrong about it being reasonable. All the police forces are riddled with spies."

"But," Evana interposed, "publicity is what you need in this case. The moment you reveal the existence of the liquid metal and Emerson's identity, he has no more reason for coming after you."

Blord laughed grimly. "And then suppose I'm called up before a lie detector and asked to explain where I got my sample of liquid metal. In case you don't know it, bribery is a criminal offense even in the Ridge Stars. No, my dear, we have two advantages over Emerson. First, we're the only ones who know his identity. Second, he can't be sure that we know. We mustn't give up either advantage lightly."

"Well," the girl shook her head, "Marian says she'll do what she can, of course, but she says not to count on your own physics lab matching science with wizards like Emerson, Ashleyton and Hounsley. And as for me, I'm very unhappy over the plan that I suspect is in your mind."

Blord studied her soberly. "My dear, this is not a case of what I want. Whatever advantage I gain will come as a result of acting without delay—"

It was two hours later that the call came through from Magrusson. "The city of Hid on the cave planet?" said Blord. "Good work. . . . I'll keep in touch with you."

Chapter 19

A shadow moved from a cave of Carnot. It flitted over a pile of rubble, then crouched behind a rock and looked down at the cave city of Hid. The city sprawled over a porous plain, its towers reaching up toward the high, overhanging ceiling of rock. There were blaze points of brightness in that massive ceiling, and a very fire of light shed down on the city below.

The shadow shimmered as it came out from behind the rock into that brilliance. Swiftly now, as it moved forward, it dissolved into the unchanging artificial brightness of the underground city. Once in the city, the invisible man lost his haste. He walked a score of streets, crossing roads to avoid the shadows of buildings, and carefully stepping aside for men and women hurrying along the sidewalks. He paused for minutes on end, listening to conversations; and, for half an hour, he stood staring up at the great central administration building, above which a spaceship floated. At last he made his way to a large showy building with several entrances. A glitter sign flared colorfully:

CHEZ MADAME
GAMES AND GIRLS

The invisible man glided lightly through one of the entrances, through an oddly empty gambling salon and along a bright corridor. There was a key in a clever little contrivance beside one of the doors. The door opened into an imposing apartment. In a leisurely fashion, he went to one of the bedrooms, and took off the invisibility suit. He had just lain down on the bed when the key clicked again in the outer lock.

A woman's voice said, "Oooohh!" Footsteps sounded. The bedroom door was pushed open, and a buxom, motherly-looking, fifty-year-old woman came rushing in. "Artur," she said. "Artur, it's you! Or rather—" she smiled affectionately— "the flesh mask version of you that you let me see."

Artur Blord said: "I'm glad you're glad to see me, Kate."

"Artur," she said heavily, "You're not kidding. Glad is a tiny word for the way I feel. Crime doesn't pay any more, at least not in Hid. A month ago, this city was taken over. The new men killed the Seven of Hid, including Boss Tanser They just laughed at our defenses; at our weapons, which were designed to hold off any attack the space patrol might make if it discovered there was an underground city here."

She sighed wearily. "Artur, I'd like you to get me out of here. They've lengthened the working hours to twelve a day. They've got all the factories running on shifts, and all the men who were in hiding here are in them, chained to machines, turning out good work or else. My business is all shot to pieces."

Artur Blord was frowning. "What are they manufacturing?"

"Instruments!"

"What kind?"

"I only know about the ones here. Just imagine, my own place put into a mechanical strait jacket. The devices are just inside the doors and windows, and they look me and my customers over when we come in or go out."

"Look you over?" Sharply.

"They're some kind of an X-ray machine. They compare the shape of my bones and my insides with a previous record

93

inside the machine. They make sure I'm me— What's the matter?"

Blord was on his feet, struggling to pull his invisibility suit from under the bed, where he had put it. The woman stared at him, startled. Abruptly, alarm came into her thick, jolly face.

"Oh, space!" she muttered. "One of those seeing-eye things must have registered *you* when you came in."

There was a heavy pounding on the corridor door. Blord shrugged, pushed the invisibility suit under the bed again, and accepted the handcuffs a few minutes later without resistance.

He was taken straight to the administrative center. As he was led into an elevator, Blord was thinking tensely: The important thing was to keep his identity concealed behind his flesh mask. And remember that *they* couldn't have time to check personally every individual of a city of half a million population. Fortunately, he had taken a few mental precautions before leaving his ship. His thought slowed as the elevator stopped. He was led along plush-covered corridors to a door marked:

CITY DIRECTORY

Inside was a large office with several hundred girl clerks at various machines and, to one side, a long series of booths. A young woman came forward, then motioned Blord's escort to lead him to one of the booths, where another young woman, a blonde, sat behind a desk. The first woman went away.

"Have you searched him?" asked the blonde briskly.

The job was done then and there. It was thorough, in a surfacy kind of way. It removed his shoulder gun, his sleeve blaster, and his three electronically treated knives. It took his pocketbook, the extra money in the lining of his coat, and his shoes with their hollowed heels and soles. It failed to test his teeth, or the buttons on his coat, nor did it locate the variety of transparent drugs under his fingernails and toenails. When it was finished, he was motioned into a chair opposite the blonde; and the interview began.

His name? He gave that as Len Christopher. His occupation? None!

"Nothing at all?" Sharply.

"Oh, I just sort of move around," said Blord in his most transparent, evasive manner.

She wrote down, "Thief."

It seemed to Blord that it was time he made a protest. "Say, listen," he began in his best underground whine. "What goes on around here? I come to Hid in my usual manner, and what do I find—an organized city."

The girl smiled grimly. "There have been a few changes. By what route did you come here?"

"I ain't sayin'," said Blord.

Out of the corner of his eye, he saw the fist of one of his escorts smashing toward him. He took the blow moving away, and so it merely stunned him. But he lay back as if he had been knocked out, and let them pour water on him to himself, and they've taken over the administration building. revive him. He shook his head dizzily. The woman said coolly, "We like answers to our questions."

Blord said sullenly: "A friend o' mine put me down in one of the caves that comes into Hid at the north. Took me about two hours to walk in." Actually, he had come in from the south. But he was a badly worried man. He thought in dismay: "What have I run into?"

The young woman said, "Take him over to the map."

It was an ordinary three-dimensional map of the caves; and Blord knew them all well. Their outlets in the barren surface of the planet and most of their capillary off-shoots and dead ends had long ago been hypnotically impressed upon his brain. Looking at them, Blord hesitated. It was not impossible that some of the entrances had had "seeing" instruments concealed in them. It made the problem of lying difficult.

"They look," he temporized, "kind of funny, seen like this."

"Which one?" said the cold-voiced young woman.

Blord decided on the truth. The important thing was that he mustn't be brought before Emerson or Ashleyton or the others. No other danger could be as great as the thorough examination such men would give him. The cave by which he had entered couldn't have an all-coverage "seeing" device in it as yet, because he hadn't been arrested until he crossed the threshold of the Chez Madame. After he had indicated the southern cave by which he had entered, the young woman said:

"All this of course will be verified by the lie detector."

"Whaddaya think I'm tellin' the truth for?" said Blord. "I can recognize a solid set-up when I'm in it."

He was feeling easier now. His conviction that individual cases *must* be left to subordinates had proved correct. As for lie detectors, that at least he had prepared for. He was doped to the hilt by mechanical hypnosis.

"And now," said the woman, "where have you been staying since you arrived?"

"Oh, I just got here today," said Blord. And realized from the look on her face that he had blundered.

"Today?" said the young woman in surprise. "Why, that's impossible. No one has come from outside for eight days without setting off the alarms." She twisted to look up at the men. "Take this fellow," she commanded, "to see the chief of directory. I think he's lying, but orders are to have all doubtful cases checked by number three."

Five minutes later, Blord was standing stiffly in front of the famous Professor Ashleyton. Before the scientiest had time to say anything, a door opened and Brian Emerson walked in. The arrival of the great man was an accident, Blord was convinced. But the coincidence chilled him. In all his career, chance had seldom worked so hard and so often against him.

Emerson walked over behind Ashleyton and glanced down at Blord's "Len Christopher" record, which Ashleyton was reading. The action gave Blord time to examine the two scientists. Both were wearing flesh masks. But Blord had studied their three-dimensional motion picture images until he could recognize the very way in which they stood or sat, the slight stoop of Ashleyton's shoulders, the deep chest of Emerson. Ashleyton was tall and thin, with bony fingers and an elongated head. Emerson was tall and big, his face square and massive. The man radiated physical and nervous strength.

Looking at him and Ashleyton, Blord felt a morbid thrill. Suddenly, the situation seemed fantastic. It was one thing to sit in his office and analyze the presence of these men here in the Ridge Stars from the scanty data he had had. It was quite another to see them in the environment of Hid, men who had a short time before been honored and responsible citizens— now acting their chosen role of super-pirates.

Emerson laughed, a thick, guttural, confident laugh. "It would be interesting to know, Christopher," he said, "which of the three possible methods you used in getting by our temporary alarm system. Was it an invisibility suit or—" He stopped. "Never mind. By the time you get back here the coverage will be complete." He shrugged. "You're a lucky man. Under normal conditions, you would already be working at a machine in one of the factories of Hid. But instead we are going to send you to Delfi II."

"Huh!" said Blord. "What for?" He was genuinely surprised.

Emerson shrugged. "The skill with which you came into this city impresses me, and I haven't been impressed very much recently. In fact, I've been disgusted with the human material I have to work with— But now, I presume you've heard of Artur Blord?"

Blord waited, wondering what was coming, a tiny bit uneasy at this mention of his own name.

Emerson continued: "One of our first acts will be to take over the Blord empire."

Blord said, "You're going to what?"

He began to laugh, then checked it quickly. He said derisively, "Listen, boss, you go after Blord and you'll eat dirt so fast you won't ever know what hit you."

97

Emerson made no immediate reply. The smile had faded from his face, but there was a faint contempt in his expression as he said in a flat, unemotional voice, "Artur Blord will be dead in two weeks, because he knows, or is on the point of knowing, something about me. And my plan against him includes the taking over of his entire organization. But enough of this," he said curtly. "Your instructions, Christopher, will be given you when you leave. And now, hand me that syringe, Ashleyton."

One look at the yellowish substance in the transparent tube of the syringe, and Blord knew the worst. It had become clear that Emerson's presence in Ashleyton's office was not accident. The blonde in City Directory must have advised Ashleyton that a resourceful thief was being sent up, and Ashleyton in turn had called Emerson for *this* purpose. Unobtrusively as possible, Blord started his left hand up toward his mouth. If he could swallow the drug under his middle fingernail— To cover his intention, he said nervously, "What are you going to do to me, Boss?"

Emerson laughed again. "This is what is known as seven-day poison. In its primitive state, which is the only version on the general market, it reacts chemically with the blood, and kills on the seventh day. But those who fully understand the complex protein structure of the poison can vary the time lapse between injection and death to some extent. This particular mixture, for instance, is set to kill on the thirtieth day. There are only two antidotes. One of them must have the original poison mixture as a base. Fortunately, it can be administered any time up to the moment before death." Emerson smiled. "Since we are keeping that mixture here, you will readily see the importance of carrying out our instructions to the letter. To save your life you will have to return to Hid for an antidote."

He paused. He seemed to be secretly amused. Then, "The second antidote has to be taken in advance. Clever men frequently carry a dose under their fingernails. *Grab his arm!*" The professor laughed with a throaty triumph. "No, no, my friend. Tricks like that don't work with us. Roll up his sleeve!"

The needle made a brief pain in Blord's arm.

"That's all," said Emerson. "Take him to transportation."

Chapter 20

After an hour, the council of war in Blord's office had still got nowhere. Blord studied the faces of the one man and four women. For the first time in his life, he had a curious feeling about these people who worked for him. He felt remote, aloof, dissociated. The poison made a difference in outlook. He examined the faces more closely, with a new awareness of the fact that his organization had a preponderance of women. Funny that men who came to the Ridge Stars could never be completely trusted in a subordinate position.

Evana Travis was saying with a quiet confidence, "I'm sure Artur will think of something."

Blord mustered a wry smile for her. But all he said was, "Not once after I was captured did I have a real chance of doing anything on my own, and my final release had nothing to do with any personal skill. Nor, considering the poison, was it actually final. Whatever plan we work out must include my return to Hid to a *living* Emerson and Ashleyton, to get the antidote injection."

There was silence. The three women scientists looked at each other. Sarah Gray, chemist, said at last with a sigh, "Your predicament greatly limits any planning we might do." She added, "You haven't told us yet what instructions Emerson gave you. Perhaps we could lay a trap."

Blord smiled wearily. The suggestion was typical of what

this meeting had so far produced: vague, ordinary, unimaginative, almost defeatist. He said, "Here's the catch to that, Sarah. At eleven o'clock on March 28th, that's nine days from now, I'm supposed to beam my information on an individual sender, which they supplied me. Try to lay a trap with that set-up."

"But what information do they want?" Sharply, urgently, Marian Clark, the chief of his science staff, who had first brought him the liquid metal, asked the question.

"I'm supposed to learn something about the movements of Artur Blord," said Blord, "and report to Hounsley, their communications man."

Magrusson, the only other man in the room, wiped the sweat off his heavy face. "I hope," he said, "that they don't get the idea of blasting this building."

Blord smiled at the general manager. The other's gloom made him suddenly more cheerful. "Don't worry about your skin, old man. Emerson has spectacular ideas, and one of them is to take over all my properties. He'll need you to manage them."

"But—" said Magrusson wildly.

"Don't ask me," said Blord, "how he's going to work it. That's what's worrying me. If he can take over my estate, then the galactic legal system is worthless. Just suppose I get killed. Of course," he went on, "everybody in this room is in my will. And some eight dozen families scattered throughout the Ridge Stars, as well as some others, altogether, about a thousand people." He smiled, "This split-up isn't as bad as it sounds. I'm sure even Magrusson has no clear idea of my total wealth. I own whole cities. On some planets every factory, every power plant, every mine belongs to me."

He broke off, "My will is registered on the Registered Circuit, supposedly a foolproof mechanical device, so much so that every deal great or small, on Earth and elsewhere, is dependent upon its inviolability." His face darkened. "I am going to assume that not even Ashleyton can alter anything already registered on the Circuit. However, he might be able to add something."

Magrusson moaned softly. "Everything has been going wrong lately. First, that scoundrel, Philips, pulls his stuff again and again, and—"

Blord interrupted him. "I see," he said bleakly, "that we'll have to think this business over."

The meeting broke up in a dead silence.

On the third day after the meeting, Blord was at the main physics laboratory. "This liquid metal," he asked Marian Clark, "how does it work?"

The woman physicist said, "In liquid metal, the normal crystalline tension is relaxed by the removal of the gravitons. The metal flows in a molecular stream but—and this is what makes the process so important—it greedily absorbs gravitons from the nearest layer, thus setting off a chain of liquefying reactions. But some of the gravitons are radiated in the form of gravitic energy—that hissing sound you heard—and therefore it takes about an hour before a newly liquefied piece of metal returns to its solid state."

She broke off eagerly, "Have you got an idea about the metal—against Emerson?"

Blord shook his head. "I haven't got a single thought," he confessed.

Two days later, Blord was back at the laboratory, this time accompanied by a gloomy Evana.

"I'm puzzled," Blord began. "Suppose Emerson came up to my office to kill me, and as the door opened he was met by every conceivable type of weapon fire. Mind you, that won't happen. I can't afford to have him killed until I have the poison antidote. But he doesn't know that, and therefore will expect that I have a defensive system. Is there anything known in science that would help him?"

The woman physicist looked at him steadily. "Not *known*," she said at last. But about seven years ago, a rumor started on Earth to the effect that an EGS scientist had developed a basic counterant to all radiant guns. Rumor had it that the counterant reversed the flow of power, which invariably resulted in the destruction of the gun and, of course, its wielder. We put all our spies in EGS, including Hounsley, on the job, but all they could report was that several important scientists had died suddenly. The rumor remained just that."

When she had finished, Blord said, "You know, I can see now that you were right, originally. I've been approaching this whole problem from the wrong angle. You warned me, remember, not to count on our science to match that of Emerson and Ashleyton. And there's no question of it. For ten years, he's had the pick of the inventions of more than ninety thousand EGS scientists. On his own ground, he's undefeatable."

"You mean you've got an idea?" Evana said, brightening.

Frowning, Blord shook his head. "I'll have to think it over. My materials are men and their psychology. My methods are tricks. I should have thought of that before. There must be something—"

The sixth and seventh days he had no ideas. On the eighth day Blord sat in his office thinking in a shocked wonder. Was it possible that he was really beaten? The thought ended as Magrusson and Evana came in. The plump man's face was longer than usual.

"I've got a carload of trouble for you," he began darkly. "How would you like it—in pieces, or all in one lump?"

Blord laughed. He couldn't help it. The man was too gloomy. To Magrusson, life was so serious a business that it took all his energy to keep from sinking into a state of permanent depression.

The general manager snarled, "You're a fine one. Tomorrow we may all be dead, and you think it's funny."

With an effort, Blord ended his amusement. He sat back in his chair, more relaxed than he had felt in many days. "Thanks," he said at last. "I needed that. Go ahead and tell me anything you want."

"First," said Magrusson bleakly, "there's Philips again. His latest—"

Evana caught the look on his face and said quickly, "He means the Philips who's been impersonating you."

Blord scarcely heard. He felt warm with excitement. "Philips!" he said delightedly. "Why, of course. He's the answer.

How could I have neglected to include Philips, since he insists upon including himself?"

He was on his feet now, the sparkle back in his dark eyes. "Magrusson," he cried, "get Philips up here. Tell him we'll agree to his blackmail. Tell him anything. But get him here!"

The general manager stared at him gloomily. "You must be crazy," he said. "Have you forgotten that you've still got to go to Hid? What makes you think Emerson will even bother to give you the antidote?"

"He'll give it to me," said Artur Blord savagely, "in order to save his own life."

"It sounds pretty dangerous to me," said the general manager.

"Of course it's dangerous," snapped Blord. "It's danger that makes life interesting." He broke off. "What a fool I've been. The psychology of this business has been plain from the beginning: Hounsley—Philips!"

"The real danger," said Magrusson with sudden insight, "and the main trouble with you, is that you admire men like Emerson. I'll bet you're going to let him live."

Blord scarcely heard. He was laughing harshly, "The Philips part is going to be pretty sordid, but he's been asking for it."

Artur Blord was dead. Accidentally killed by the explosion of his own electron blaster. According to the police, he must have taken it out of his holster for some idle purpose, and it short-circuited.

On Delfi II, the news spread rapidly. Crowds gathered at the foot of the two-hundred-story Blord Building, and stared curiously up at the remote penthouse where the accident had happened. The news flashed by eldophone through the Ridge Stars, and raced on to Earth and to the remoter stars beyond. His fame was surprising. Everywhere public eldoplates and newspapers carried the picture of his dead body, almost torn in two, and lying in a great pool of vividly red blood at the foot of his desk.

It was not a good picture, aside from its horror. It showed

his face too clearly. And there was a half snarl on that distinctive countenance that suggested that, at the instant of death, an unpleasant and hitherto concealed characteristic of the famous operator had stamped its soulless imprint on his face. A strange, wolfish Blord lay dead in that palatial private office. The picture shocked millions of his admirers, and several newspapers commented editorially on the fact.

Most papers and commentators, however, were generous with their praise. His fantastic exploits were told in detail. And the papers quoted with genuine pleasure the statement of General Manager Magrusson that, "I didn't even know he was in his office. I thought he was somewhere out at the other end of the Ridge Stars. But that's the way he was. He came and went like a ghost." To the end, the newspapers pointed out, he had lived his strange, dramatic life to the full.

On the fifth day, interest switched to a new angle of the case: The Blord fortune! Newspapers were expansive in their estimates of its extent. A trillion stellors was the smallest figure printed; and, as the tidal waves of esimates grew, the question began to be asked: Who were the heirs?

On the seventh day, the director-general of the Registered Circuit arrived from Fasser IV, and issued a cautious statement to the effect that there were two wills, one made only a week before Blord's death, which completely superseded the earlier one. It was a perfectly legal will, and it left the entire Blord fortune to one, Johann Smith, who was staying at the Blord hotel. Upon this hotel, reporters descended *en masse*.

They were granted an interview by a man of magnetic personality who bore a suspicious physical, though not facial resemblance to Professor Brian Emerson—but no one noticed that—and who issued a statement to the effect that, "I once saved Artur Blord's life. I am leaving the case in the hands of my lawyers and the courts. I'll come back when the legal situation is straightened out."

The next day he had disappeared.

Chapter 21

There were ways, Artur Blord knew, of getting into Hid that no group of professors, newly arrived from Earth, could possibly have discovered. These entrances—and exits—were not dangerous to Hid in its role as a hiding place. But for simple purposes, such as the movement of careful individuals, they served very well indeed. They had been built by the former Boss Tanser for emergency use. And Blord's coordination department had paid a large sum to a Tanser henchman for the secret.

Blord arrived invisible, mainly because there were certain things he had to do, one man he had to kill. He did so, coolly, without mercy. Then, all sense of haste gone, he walked along the streets of a transformed Hid. The city's boulevards were crowded with sleekly dressed men and women. The gambling houses swarmed with players and, as doors opened and shut, the streets echoed with laughter and the clinking of glasses, the sound of whirring wheels and the calls of the croupiers. Blord had brief glimpses of flashing interior lights, and a sustained view of miles of dazzling streets signs.

Here was the old Hid, with something added. The playground hideout of a hundred thousand wanted criminals, waiting for the police to forget. A score of conversations listened to, gave Blord the picture. The feverish factory work into which everyone had been forced, was over. The frightened crooks, discovering that their labor had been designed for the whole purpose of strengthening the defenses of Hid, were so relieved that their reaction was admiration for the new city bosses. The talk along the boulevards was that, in future, Hid would be the base for gigantic operations. There was an overall excitement that infected individuals. They shouted oftener, laughed louder, and gambled more recklessly. Everywhere was a feeling of great things in the offing.

Blord felt justified once more in his over-all plan. If it worked, the Ridge Stars would be saved from an era of unequalled crime. Grim with the potentialities, he departed at last the way he had come—and a few hours later entered Hid by the more regular route he had used a few weeks before.

As he emerged, a force struck him, pinioned his arms, and catapulted him at express speed along a gravitic line. The speed lessened after a few seconds, and he could see his destination: a car, one of several, on a track. He was dropped into it lightly. Instantly, still without human intervention, the car raced off across a barren field toward the city. During the entire trip, his hands and feet were held in an energy rise. Abruptly, the car rushed into a tunnel and came to a stop inside a steel cage.

Lounging men sprang toward the car, released him from his bondage and took him up to City Directory. It was a different girl and a different booth this time, but Blord did not wait for the interview. He said coolly, "You may tell Number One that Artur Blord would like to see him." That brought results.

They were waiting for him in a large room, a dozen men, standing in small groups, talking in low tones. They turned as he entered, handcuffed, his four guards alertly surrounding him. Emerson came forward, frowning. He waved the guards out of the room.

"If you're really Blord," he said, "I must say I admire your nerve but not your intelligence."

Blord smiled. "I'm afraid, Emerson, you'll have to admire that too, before I'm finished."

"Emerson!" exclaimed Emerson.

There was a stirring in the background. A man exclaimed. "He knows us."

A brief silence settled over the room. The former EGS professors, with the exception of Emerson, stood tense, eyes narrowed, their minds obviously racing over the possibilities of the identification. Emerson alone seemed strengthened by the revelation. He smiled. Then he laughed a throaty, chuckling laugh. "This is a good one," he said. "So we caught Artur Blord in our trap a few weeks ago, and didn't know it." His laughter ended on a curt note. "You silly fool," he said. "You could have got away without a suspicion on our part. I fully intended to give you the antidote."

"I believe that," said Blord, "which is why I'm going to let you remain alive."

The words had a chilling effect. Emerson drew back, stiffening. "I'm not sure," he said slowly, "that I'm amused any more. Who was that chap in your office who drew his gun on Ashleyton and myself when we went there to kill you?"

"Do you mind if I sit down?" Blord asked. He did not wait for an answer, but walked over to the nearest chair. The moment he was seated, he held up his manacled hands. "And how about taking these off? They're quite unnecessary."

No one moved. "Come, come," said Blord sharply, "I've been thoroughly searched. My clothes have been changed, my fingernails and toenails scraped, my false tooth removed. My victory over you has nothing to do with any action that I personally can take against you. I expect intelligent understanding of such details."

There was a pause. Then Emerson called the guards. "Release him," he said grimly.

When the guards had gone, Emerson said, "Start talking. First, that fellow in your office?"

"Philips was his name," said Blord without hesitation. "He's been going around the Ridge Stars, impersonating me, his purpose being blackmail. I thought I'd let him find out that being Artur Blord isn't all gravy. And you didn't give him a chance to talk." His voice became very quiet. "I saw the death scene in a film that was taken of the whole affair. Very interesting."

Emerson was cold, cold and deadly. "It is indeed interesting," he said from between clenched teeth. "I suppose you

107

realize that you are completely at our mercy, and that we will get every scrap of information in your brain. Particularly, we will find out who else knows how much, what precautions you have taken, and other related items."

Blord was shaking his head, smiling. "It isn't as simple as that, I'm afraid. You see, I have a basic advantage over you: I have no fear of death. That sounds odd, I know. People have an idea that because I own a quarter of the Ridge Stars, which, by the way, is an exaggeration, I have everything to live for. They're wrong. I've *had* everything that life has to offer. To me, the only moments that matter are moments like this, and even they are beginning to pall."

Emerson said steadily, "We have yet to hear a single word of concrete evidence from you."

Blord ignored the interruption. But his smile had faded. He leaned forward tensely. He said, "All this is a preamble to the following statement: It is easy for a man who does not fear death and who has unlimited money to deal in bribery, corruption and the fear of death in others. I am thinking particularly of your colleague, Professor Hounsley, who used to take bribes from me, and who is not, please notice, in this room. Nor will a call to where you think he is do any good."

It would have been hard, Blord reflected, after he had spoken the words, for Hounsley to be anywhere in a coherent state. Dead men didn't turn up at gatherings.

Coolly, then, he explained his terms.

A week later, back on Delfi II, Blord felt the difference in the atmosphere of his office. This time the four women were all smiles. Even Magrusson's moon face was a shade less gloomy.

"It was all really quite simple," Blord said immodestly. "I had to die realistically to find out if Emerson really could get around the Registered Circuit, which is the very basis of our contract and legal system. It turned out that all he could do was insert a skillfully forged will."

After a pause, he went on, "While Ashleyton and Emerson were in my office killing Philips, I called Hounsley on the sender Emerson had given me. I offered him one hundred million stellors to let me see the secrets aboard the experimental ship, *Creative Physics*. Figures like that always stagger the minds of men, and it is amusing to make such offers even when you have no intention of paying.

"Hounsley was shocked when he discovered I was still alive, and I knew I had him when Emerson came to Delfi II under the name of Johann Smith to claim my property. It was obvious that Hounsley had failed to report my conversation with him. Perhaps he intended to betray me. I don't know. I arrived in Hid on the day it was his turn to look after the *Creative Physics,* and killed him the moment he let me aboard."

Blord stopped at that point and looked questioningly at Magrusson. "What's the matter?"

The plump man said, "How is it that Hounsley wasn't wearing one of those devices that explode all firearms in reverse?"

"Oh, he was wearing one all right," Blord said. "I choked him to death, so I wasn't really interested in his mechanical defenses. Physically, he was picayune."

"Oh!" said Magrusson.

Blord went on, "As soon as I was in control, I let Marian and Sarah aboard. And the rest was simply a matter of letting Emerson know that there was a ship floating above that was ready to level the whole city of Hid. I gave them my usual line about not being afraid to die. They knew *they* were, so—" He laughed with genuine glee.

Evana was shaking her head. "I can't understand," she said, "why you let Emerson and the others remain alive."

Blord stared at her. "My dear," he said, "I really don't kill any more than I have to. I couldn't of course take a chance on Hounsley being alive when Marian and Sarah were alone on the ship. But if I started to exterminate all the men in the Ridge Stars who deserve it, I'd have to build a gun as big as Earth's moon, and blow up every planet in the Ridge Stars.

"Besides," he went on, "the professor, now that he has

been shorn of his main secrets, should prove a colorful addition to my file on big operators of the Ridge Stars."

He finished thoughtfully, "Emerson, of course, is a megalomaniac. Sooner or later, he'll come after me again; and then I may have to kill him. Meanwhile, I can't afford to let the prospect frighten me, so—" He smiled "—I'll just forget about it!"

Chapter 22

Evana Travis listened with quiet thoughtfulness as Artur Blord talked.

"The trouble," he was saying, "is that nothing can really happen any more in the Ridge Stars. Every day the Artur Blord Holding Company does several ten millions of stellors' worth of business, but it's all cut and dried now. Even the crooks who try to cheat us conform to trite formulas."

Evana said quietly: "Only eight months have passed since Emerson nearly killed you."

Blord went on as if he had not heard the interjection: "Take the Corbett case that Magrusson has been pushing at me the last few days. The old stuff. Disloyal male employee. Responsible position as buyer. For years he's been buying goods from firms that paid him a commission on the side. I wouldn't think of prosecuting him except for one thing. He let them sell him shoddy goods. That's unforgivable."

As he paused for breath, the eldophone on his desk began to buzz softly, and the blue light of an interstellar call made a haze of color above the light cup.

"So far as I can see," said Blord, his hand on the phone, "I have exhausted all the possibilities for excitement in the

Ridge Star group." He picked up the receiver. "Artur Blord speaking," he said.

A scene of deep space darkened the eldophone plate. There was a spaceship in the distance, and off to one side a red point of light. Blord frowned. "What th—" he said.

An urgent voice cut him off. "Mr. Blord, this is Captain Gary, of your freighter, *Zand*. I have just been fired on by the ship you see."

Blord said grimly, "Fire back. And get that body out there. It's a human being, if the red color isn't fooling us."

"That's what I wanted to know, sir. I guess they didn't see me at first. They tossed the body out, and I saw the red point on the plate."

The advantage was with Captain Gray. The other ship had catapulted the human being into space while proceeding at speed. At the last instant, those aboard must have become aware of the ship behind them. They were striving now to turn around, and great flashes of energy poured at both the moving red dot that was a human being, and at the *Zand*. The situation was basically intolerable. With two ships firing atomic energy at each other, the incident had to be over swiftly. The ending was double-barreled. The *Zand* flashed up to the dead body. Tractor beams drew it into the air lock. And simultaneously, the stranger ship turned tail and ran at top acceleration. It was instantly out of sight as a ship, although its yellow glimmer continued on the eldoplate for several minutes.

Blord said softly, "Good work, Captain. You'll get a bonus for yourself and your crew. Give me the data as soon as you have any." He leaned back in his chair, and sighed. "Imagine," he said to Evana, "I'm down to this stuff. A petty murder of some kind. What was it Lane Stetson, the patrol commissioner from Marmora, said to me the other day?— There are nine thousand known murders committed every month in the Ridge Stars. That wouldn't normally include the attempted murder we just saw. Most killings in space merely result in the person involved being listed as 'missing' and—"

He was interrupted. Captain Gray's face came onto the

screen for the first time. It was a rough-hewn countenance, darkened by the glare of many suns. The officer said gravely, "I'm sorry to report, Mr. Blord, that there are no obvious identifying marks, but he was shot before he was thrown into space. They didn't take any chances."

"Oh," said Blord. He made no further comment. But actually his interest in the affair began at that moment.

It was about nine hours later when Blord's yacht matched velocity with the *Zand*. A few minutes later, he and his experts climbed aboard the freighter, and the investigation began.

With bleak eyes, Blord stared down at the dead man. About forty years old, he thought. An intelligent face, sensitive, confident—that was important. Not even the certainty of death had shaken the innate confidence of this man. Such people were never completely untraceable in two hundred planetfuls of nonentities. Somewhere there would be a record of his personality. The photographer was pressing toward the body, and so Blord stepped back. The movement brought him to the side of Captain Gray, and Blord felt impelled to explain his presence.

"Two things aroused my interest," he said. "They made such determined efforts to destroy the corpse. And they risked their own lives for several minutes in a gun duel to prevent ·you from getting the body. My conclusions are simple." He paused for a moment, then went on, "The killers are tough, experienced scoundrels who, normally, would do a thorough job of destroying identifying marks on their victims, and let it go at that. The fact that they were not satisfied in this case with ordinary precautions indicates that it's an important murder. The first evidence that I'm right will be that we'll find nothing on the body that will help us to identify it. I'll bet on that."

He won his hypothetical bet. Two men literally took the clothes of the corpse to pieces in their search for clues. They abandoned the effort finally, and one said, "The cloth is a common artificial wool. Billions of yards are sold every year. Without tailor marks, it's impossible to trace."

He shrugged, and he was not the only one. The X-ray man said with the anger of frustration, "The fool was in perfect health. Never had a tooth filled or out. Never had a surgeon cut into him. Won't people ever realize that the patrol has complete records of operations and injuries available at a moment's notice by automatic-electronic comparison?"

Apparently, the same kind of fools made sure that the patrol had no record of their fingerprints. Earlier, Blord had had the captain eldophoto the fingerprints to Evana, and had her route them through office channels, the pretense being that a checkup was being made on a new employee. Before he reached the *Zand,* the patrol head office—which was friendly to him—had already reported: "No record."

Now, Blord stepped to the corpse and carefully examined the smashed head. The beam of energy had entered the head just in front of the right ear, and had torn through the brain, emerging from the left temple. Death must have been instantaneous, but the direction of the wound was interesting in itself. Satisfied, Blord drew away, and motioned for the body to be covered.

"Evidently," he said, "he was shot just before being shoved into space. Shot from slightly behind and to one side. Whoever shot him couldn't know for sure that that in itself was a fatal injury, because the blow from the energy gun must have helped to knock him out into space."

He paused, scowling. But there was no escaping the fact that, for the moment at least, his hope must be that the killers would take further action. As time passed, and memory grew dim, the murderer's doubts would increase.

"We must assume," Blord said with a grim smile, "that he'll try to find out for sure. Now, we all know that a human being—because of the complete absence of pressure—would suffer internal hemorrhages the moment he was thrust out into space. But these people may not have been too careful. Maybe they didn't check to see if possibly their victim was wearing a transparent emergency spacesuit next to his skin. Under ordinary circumstances, that would scarcely matter.

But since he was picked up so quickly, they'll start wondering: "Is he alive? Is he not alive?"

He went on more thoughtfully: "And, since they undoubtedly tuned in on Captain Gray's eldophone talk with me, they know where to look for the information." He paused again, but this time there was a gleam of anticipation in his dark eyes. "We'll make up somebody to look like the dead man." His lips tightened. "And I know just the man who will be glad to volunteer for the job. A former buyer of mine named Corbett."

Blord settled his yacht into its cradle of forces atop the two-hundred-story Blord Building. Then he jumped down to the garden and walked into his penthouse office. His entrance caught Evana in the act of rising from the chair behind his desk. She looked startled as she saw him, then she smiled. "I have some messages for you," she said brightly, and vanished into her own office.

She came back a few minutes later, wondering nervously if he would ask her what she had been doing at his desk. She saw, relieved, that he was already immersed in the messages she had brought. Still quivering, she returned to her own office and sat down. Gradually, a glow spread along her nerves.

"I've succeeded," she thought, "where even he has so far failed. I've found out at least one important fact about the murder."

It had happened accidentally. She was passing through Blord's office, and it was a chance glance up at the enormous three-dimensional wall map of the Ridge Stars that brought the idea in one flash of insight. An instant later, she switched on the map lights and was sitting in Blord's chair where the map controls were located.

She kept shifting the viewpoint. The map was a size variant, so that the onlooker could have the illusion of withdrawing into remote space, and thus see all of the two-hundred-odd stars from every possible angle. Or else he could approach so close to any particular sun that it filled the entire map field. She took prolonged aims along the lines of sight,

114

and each time swiftly noted down the names of the stars that came into the line, in separate columns. Her insight was soundly rooted in logic. Captain Gray and the stranger had been travelling in the same direction before the stranger started to turn. Now, obviously, the mystery ship was both going somewhere and coming from somewhere, and one of those directions might be important to know.

Two main courses quickly dominated the welter of possible routes. First, the direction from which the enemy was coming. The suns in line were Lanvery, Leprechaun, Lorelei— She stopped there, because, "Lorelei. Why, of course, Lorelei."

Chapter 23

Blord didn't get to that stage until three days later. After dark on that third day, his protective agents brought in the disguised Corbett, and a big-toothed individual who sullenly gave his name as Slikes. Slikes admitted, since he had been caught in the attempt, that he had tried to kill Corbett. He seemed to have an idea that no further information would be extracted from him. But he was wrong.

After the interview, Blord nodded curtly to the ex-buyer. "All right, Corbett, you've done your share. If you will go to Magrusson you will receive a written release, the company will forswear all right to sue you, and will make no effort to recover from you the money you accepted as bribery when you were one of our purchasing agents." Blord paused, studying the other curiously. "By the way, how much did you make out of your connection with us?"

"Ninety million stellors," said the lean-built Corbett jauntily, and sauntered out of the office.

Blord turned to Slikes. "It looks as if this time crime is going to pay all around. Luckily, you talked, so I'm going to put you on one of my Earthbound freighters with a thousand stellors and permission to get off anywhere you want after the ship leaves the Ridge Star group."

When the hired killer had been taken away, Blord examined the information he had secured. It wasn't much, but in one sense it was everything. Whoever had hired the man, had accepted as a fact that a dead man was alive. He had given Slikes the name of his victim. Out of all that vast universe of stars, with its billions of inhabitants, a name had come out of nothingness, and the immediate rest would surely be simple.

It was. Who was Professor Philip Amand King? In twenty minutes, the central library of Suderea had the information, with an unmistakable photograph, and a life history which described the professor as the expert on the dead zone of the Lorelei sun.

"Lorelei," said Blord aloud, explosively, after he had broken the connection, "why, of course, Lorelei."

He buzzed for Evana and told her briefly what he had discovered, and what he wanted. The girl nodded and went out smiling. An hour later she brought him the typed sheets that she had had ready for nearly seventy-two hours. There were three separate sheets. The first one read:

During the past two years thirty-seven freighters have been caught by Lorelei. Altogether, in the history of the Ridge Stars, one hundred and ninety-two ships were lured to destruction by this sun, and there is no question that those lost previous to five years ago were accident. In the opinion of our transport department, the total of the last few years is not so out of proportion as it appears to be. Space traffic has jumped a hundred-fold since the introduction of the locally owned space drive a few years ago. All spaceship repair services have been overstrained and the resulting inefficiency is believed responsible for the disasters.

The second page said:

Of the thirty-seven vessels recently caught by Lorelei, six were serviced by us, seventeen by Squire and Blakely, four by the Corliss Company, and two each by the following named firms.

The list of company names appended. The third and last page was brief:

Professor Philip King, who was doing research on the problem, has been missing from his Fasser IV home for a month. There is no record that he or anyone else had discovered a method of entering the dead zones of Lorelei.

Blord put down the papers and looked up at the girl. "The way I see it, Evana," he said, "is that Professor King invented a Lorelei zone meter and then allowed himself to be inveigled into using it illegally. That is, for salvaging vessels already caught by Lorelei. That's not too hard to understand. The law allows salvagers only fifty percent. King and his group would get one hundred percent. Then King discovered that the group was actually luring new vessels into the zone. At that point he balked, and was promptly killed. The killers think he's still alive. But they're assuming that he hasn't dared say anything because, after all, he's guilty of a crime too. And now," he stood up and said briskly, "I want you to investigate the Squire & Blakely Spaceship Service and Repair Corporation. I consider it suspicious that seventeen of the ships recently caught by Lorelei should have been last serviced in their shops."

It was more than suspicious. They could have bribed mechanics in other firms to sabotage an occasional ship, as a cover-up for their own activities, but only in their own shops would the guilty firm be able to select the freighters with pay cargoes. He called after Evana as she was returning to her own office, "And check on the cargo angle, too."

He was feeling better now. He reached forward, and touched the necessary keys on the eldophone. Almost immediately, the face of Magrusson appeared on the plate. Magrusson frowned at him as he explained the situation. When Blord had finished, Magrusson said seriously, "Listen, Artur, why not let the space patrol handle it?" He must have seen the look on Blord's face for he added hastily, "Now, don't get mad. I know you don't like calling in the police on anything you've started."

Blord said, "For once, that's not the reason."

Magrusson was watching him thoughtfully, "I see," he said, "Evidence."

"Exactly," said Blord. "The possibility of a court conviction is so slim that it cannot be considered."

"But what are you going to do?"

Blord was grim. "Whoever I find is behind it, I'm going to bust wide open."

A look of alarm came into Magrusson's plump face. "Artur," he said in a voice that trembled, "you know better than to talk like that. You can't break a firm these days by any kind of pressure, financial or otherwise. The Companies Commissioner could close our entire business if you tried it."

That wasn't what he'd meant, and Blord was briefly irritated that he had been misunderstood. But the irritation fled before the grim picture Magrusson's frightened words had conjured up. He visualized the trillion stellor Blord economic empire being forcibly liquidated and a chill ran along his nerves. At last he said savagely, "I'll think of something." For several seconds he sat frowning, then he remembered his reason for calling Magrusson. "I'm leaving for Lorelei in a few minutes," he said, "and I want to give you some instructions."

Twenty minutes later he was on his way.

The following "morning"—Suderea time—Blord called up Evana. The call was still on the eldo half an hour later. He was eating breakfast when he realized that she should have replied long ago. He went into the control room, and eldophoned Magrusson.

The manager's image came on in a few seconds. "Miss Travis," he said. "Wait a minute and I'll see—" His face blurred as he talked to someone else, then grew clear again. He said succinctly, "The building guard office says she went out last night immediately after you left and she hasn't come in yet."

Blord sat silent, then slowly: "She's been acting odd these past few days."

He changed the subject. "Got that information yet?"

"Not yet. But the ships are gathering."

"O.K."

Quite a sun was Lorelei, but not visibly so. Blord pulled the cap off the eyepiece of the telescope, made a few adjustments, and looked out into the blackness. A few stars glittered palely in the remote, tremendous night. After several minutes he found the outline of the famous dark star he was looking for.

Its outstanding characteristic was that it was sixty percent helium. Helium, the "inert," long ago made sluggishly active by the hellfires that had raged around it. Not active enough ever to have explosive life of its own, but alive, nevertheless. It was a half-life of terrible instability. Like a monstrous leech, the masses of helium had sucked up all the flame energies of what had been, ages before, a blazing sun. And it hadn't been enough. Prevented by the hugeness of the space-time continuum and by its own slow speed from approaching other suns, it floated in the darkness so greedy for energy that no ship could come near it without having its electric, artificial gravitic and all radioactive energies radically reduced.

Blord's examination was briefer than he intended. He felt a sharp blow. It struck into every part of his body, and was followed instantly by an incredible lightness. In the depths of the ship, the massive atomic motors throbbed erratically—and stopped. His vision blurred. He had the sensation of swelling like a balloon as every muscle in his body fought for balance. The alarms, he thought. The Lorelei alarms and relays had failed!

His ship must have been sabotaged when it was last serviced. And so he had flown into the dead areas of Lorelei, the destroyer sun.

It took a while to explore the extent of the disaster. The yacht was falling almost directly toward the sun. Its speed, Blord remembered, had been about thirty thousand miles an hour before he had turned on the superspeed anti-gravities. Now that those greater engines were off, the machine would have reverted to its original thirty thousand miles an hour. He had about fifty tons of high explosive aboard. With that they might, just might, get his hundred-thousand-ton pleasure ship into an orbit. Nothing more.

Blord began to laugh, softly, humorlessly. He had often wondered what he would do when his time came. And here it was. He was caught by a sun that subtly strained the electronic structures of all objects in its vicinity. And the machines, dependent on delicate atomic interactions, instantly ceased to function. Theoretically, a new formula of pile arrangement could make them all work again. And, presumably, Professor King had discovered just such a formula.

The laughter faded from Blord's lips as he remembered why he was here. He began to turn a wheel that shoved at a bigger wheel which shoved at a still bigger wheel, until, under the controls dais, a ten-foot wheel with an Earth weight of fifteen tons was spinning at approximately thirty revolutions a minute. At the proper moment, Blord pushed in a clutch, and an electric dynamo began to operate.

It was very literally an emergency power plant. Electricity was too coarse an energy to be powerfully affected by the Lorelei sun. The gadget was useless as a source of interstellar drive power. But it would run for hours in gravity-free space, and, unlike the batteries which he also had for emergencies, it was capable of transmitting the eldo energies over astral distances. The power plant began to prove itself. A light flickered into existence over the eldophone, and the eldoplate began to glow. Blord adjusted the dials, and made his connection with the city of Suderea. After half a minute, Magrusson's plump face appeared on the plate.

"Hello, Artur," he said casually.

The plump man's calmness startled Blord. The sight of Magrusson, calm, normal, safe in his faraway office, made Blord sharply aware of his own tenseness. He stood for a moment, fighting back to relaxed normalcy. At last he managed a smile, but before he could speak, Magrusson said:

"I've got that information about Squire and Blakely that you wanted. Here, I'll hold up the sheets while you read. That's the quickest way."

It was quite an amazing document that Blord read then. Andrew Squire and Walter Blakely were among the less prepossessing human beings who had settled in the Ridge Stars. They were listed as having, at one time, manufactured the sex drug and the seven-day poison. Both men had been tried for murder and released because of insufficient evidence. They had practised a particularly unpleasant form of white slave trading in the remote frontier stars. Of parts of their adult life, there was no record whatever.

But age had seemingly mellowed them. Also, they had developed caution. Five years before, they had entered upon the manufacture of legal articles, branched out into spaceship repair work, and were listed in the interstellar directory as having cash and assets to the total value of three hundred million stellors. Blakely's hobby was listed as "Women." Squire's activities were covered under the more general description, "Nightclubbing."

"The funny thing," Magrusson said as Blord looked up from the last page, "is that our information center tells me Miss Travis secured all the facts in those pages nearly three days ago." He added, "She hasn't turned up yet."

Blord groaned. "She would get herself mixed up in something. Get some agents out searching for her. She's up to something but I have a feeling its too rough a deal." He added quickly:

"Where are the ships?"

"They'll be in the vicinity of Lorelei in twelve to fifteen hours." He broke off, "Artur, what's the idea behind all this?"

Blord scarcely heard the question. He was pondering the time limit, narrow-eyed and dissatisfied. In fifteen hours his battle would be won or lost, his body burned to a crisp or tossed out into the absolute zero of space. He sighed finally, and said, "What about the money? How much did you get together on such short notice?"

"Commander Jasper has fifty million stellors aboard and—" Magrusson stopped, eyes wide. "I get the set-up now, Artur! Whoever is behind the piracy will have a salvage ship on the spot. Some of the doomed vessels would plunge straight toward Lorelei, and they'd have to be stripped in a matter of days. Of course, they may have been scared off by what you discovered, but if they're bold they'll be there, and the money will attract them."

Before Blord could reply, there was a jar that nearly knocked him out of the control chair. He felt a hollow sensation in the pit of his stomach as he realized what had happened. A heavy object had bumped into the yacht.

The pirate salvage ship had arrived.

Chapter 24

Squire, of Squire and Blakely, was drunk. He leaned heavily against the bar, and only one thing was clear. This slim and friendly young woman was interested in him.

Evana Travis said, "Let's have another drink."

The man looked at her blearily. He was a short, square creature with a surprisingly clean-cut face. His eyes were narrowed the slightest bit. Drunk, he thought. And that was his good luck. He took the proffered drink. "Thanksh," he said. "But now, what were we talking about?"

"You like my idea. You're going to hire me for your company."

"That's right. Come around tomorrow. Will you let me see that little gadget again?"

Evana drew it out of her purse. It was a device called a healthograph, and it had a most interesting history, which she had no intention of telling this intoxicated man. She had secured it from the Co-ordination Department of the Blord Holding Company, a fact of which the Co-ordination Department was unaware.

"This is not the same one," she said. "I've got two. As I told you, once it's been used, it can't be used again for about twelve hours."

Squire took the device and put his fingers on the activators. He stared then, fascinated, at the dozen small dials. "Whasha matter with it?" he asked peevishly. "Why do the hands go all funny like that?"

"It needs a little work done on it. I know exactly how to fix it. If I could use your laboratories for a few weeks—"

She had to suppress a smile as she saw the look of greed come into the man's face. He licked moist lips.

"In *our* laboratory," he said. "Yes, yes, you must work out the final problem in our shop. Here"—he fumbled with a sobering intensity in his pocket—"is my card. Come and see us tomorrow."

"And don't think I won't," said Evana. "My bank account is close to rock bottom."

Next morning, she was still convinced that her plan would work. Squire and Blakely had spent their lives making money out of other people's stupidity. Surely they would accept the reality of one more sucker. She was not surprised when the desk clerk informed her that Andrew Squire had come to escort her personally to her new job.

Blakely was a bigger edition of his partner, strong looking, suave. He examined the healthograph with cruel, sleepy eyes. After he had tested himself he said with satisfaction, "Right. I had neither vitamin C nor B-1 for breakfast, and, of course, I didn't get my full quota of the others in just one meal. Oh, oh, there she goes!"

The gadget had started to register wildly, and Evana saw that Blakely was looking at her questioningly with those strange, quiet eyes. It was clear that Blakely would need a far more detailed explanation of the fault in the device than had satisfied his drunken partner. She launched into it without hesitation, as she had heard it explained to Blord by his chief physicist, weeks earlier.

The problem involved had to do with the nervous energy of the human body. This energy reacted in a subtle fashion when the system absorbed vitamins, minerals, and calories. The inventor had rightly assumed that the varying rate of absorption could be measured against either a standard requirement, or the requirements of a particular individual. In the latter case, the indicators fixing the amount needed would have to be set after a medical examination. The gadget, as originally invented, quickly became saturated with energy. It ceased to respond to subtle variations, and so became useless for about twelve hours. It was a problem in energy control that the inventor, a hundred years before, had failed to solve.

The Co-ordination Department of the Artur Blord Holding Company had rectified the energy saturation problem in less than an hour, three weeks before. It was a fact that Evana Travis neglected to mention in giving Blakely the history of the healthograph.

She could see Blakely's eyes widen ever so slightly as he realized that, while no patent could be taken out on the original invention, the improvement could be patented. "And that will not be very hard," Evana said truthfully. "The discoveries made the last few score years about the control of energy make the solution a simple matter." She realized, when she had finished, that she had made a sale.

"Order any extra equipment you need," Blakely said expansively. "We like your idea, and we play ball with those who work for us."

Evana had come prepared to be businesslike. "I'll need a

few things," she began. "If I could have a little leeway about getting equipment—"

She held out her list. Blakely did not even glance at it. He said to his partner, "Mr. Squire, will you dictate a memorandum to the Registered Circuit, authorizing Leah Carroll—" he glanced at Evana— "Have I the name correct?"

Evana nodded, and Blakely went on, "—Authorizing Leah Carroll to order equipment in our name?" After Squire and the girl had signed, Blakely faced Evana, "Satisfactory, I hope?"

They were impressing her with their openhandedness. "I can't," said Evana in her most grateful voice, "thank you enough."

When she had gone, Squire looked at Blakely. "Nice girl," he said. "A little dumb, perhaps, but—" He hesitated. "What are we going to do with her?"

His partner looked at him coldly. "What do we usually do with people who might make a nuisance of themselves if we let them live?" He paused. He fixed his pale eyes on Squire. "The moment she fixes that gadget," he said, "she dies."

Chapter 25

Sitting in the control chair, Blord had one of his rare moments of depression. Distinctly to his ears came the sound of power hammers at one of the air locks. He gazed gloomily at the image of Magrusson in the eldoplate. Artur Blord, he thought wryly, top operator in the Ridge Star area, was on his own at last. It had never before struck him how much his exploits had depended on other people and on a vast array of machines.

The dark mood passed. He said to Magrusson, "Sleep at

the office. I want to be able to get in touch with you, night or day, until further notice. And now, good-by."

He cut the connection before the other could protest. He reached up and switched off the solitary light bulb. For a moment, he sat in the darkness, one man alone. Then he caught up an electric torch and raced to the emergency cabinet. He stripped down to his skin, and put on a thin, skin-tight transparent spacesuit, all except the headpiece. Then he strapped a belt of oxygen capsules around his waist and slipped into his clothes again. A moment later, he was fumbling for the latch that swung the control chair off its base. Where the chair had been, there was a circular hole in the floor. Its tunnellike walls gleamed in the light of the torch. He lowered himself into the hole, and pulled the chair back into place with a hand lever. It locked into position with the faintest of clicks.

There was nothing wonderful or even original about the secret passageways. Their uniqueness was of a personal variety. Except for the far-off Earth firm that had built the machine, he was the only person who knew that the passageways existed.

Blord hurried along the narrow corridor until he came to a small room. At first sight, it contained no furniture at all. But Blord bent, inserted his fingers into a depression, and a chair unfolded up from the floor. Another tug, and the wall yielded a sound amplifier complete with earphones. He plugged in the electric current from the big flywheel in the adjoining room, and put on the earphones. The sound of hammering grew loud in his ears, and he had his first important information. The invaders were trying to gain entrance through air lock C-$_4$. It shouldn't take long.

It took about five minutes for the hammering to stop. Then there was a hiss, followed by the clack of metallic boots. A short pause, then, while the gangway that connected the two ships was made air-tight; and then there was a voice bellowing: "Renson and Messner, you guard the entrance. We don't want anyone sneaking into our ship. Pete!"

"Yeah, Captain Grierson?"

"Throw an energy bomb to the end of that corridor."

There was a hissing whine, then a moment's silence, which was broken by Grierson saying with satisfaction, "That'll knock out anybody with plans for an ambush. All right now. I want the ship taken in five minutes. Kill all the males, bring the females to my cabin. Each group send a man back here to report to me. Get!"

It was a victory of sorts to follow the groups by means of the amplifiers, and listen to their curses.

"No women! Nobody at all!"

A voice said, "Maybe it's an old vessel that we missed when we first started."

"Yeah," said another, "but where's the bodies. There's always been bodies before."

Blord pictured that, not for the first time. He had often had thoughts about ships caught long, long ago by the enormous dark star, Lorelei. Some of those ships must have plunged to their doom hundreds of years before, straight into the sun. Others, approaching at an angle, would have been forced into orbits, and become tiny planets, tombs for the crews and passengers aboard. There had never in the long history of the Ridge Stars been a survivor of a ship caught by Lorelei.

His thoughts were interrupted by the thunder of a furious Grierson. "What! Nobody aboard! Nonsense. Did you find out whose ship it is?"

There was a faint rustle of paper, and then silence. Evidently, someone was handing over Blord's documents to the captain. The silence grew long. It was clear that somebody was undergoing shock. At last the captain said, "Blord, eh? The great Artur Blord." The loud voice broke into laughter. "So the big shot, the man who never loses, has been caught." The laughter ended. He said something that Blord didn't catch, but there was no mistaking the response. A roar of protest broke from a score of men.

"What do you mean, take him alive?"

"We kill all these guys, don't we!"

"To hell with prisoners!"

A bellow from Grierson ended the quick opposition. He said, "This is the guy that picked up Professor King. I've got to find out for the big bosses what Blord knows about our racket here. Now, get to work and strip his ship. Get!"

Blord waited until the yacht was stripped bare, until discovery was a matter of minutes. And then he climbed out into cavernous emptiness to where Captain Grierson was directing the mobile machines that had torn a ship to pieces in ten hours.

The captain's cabin of the freighter was an untidy arrangement of chairs, desks and cabinets. There was an adjoining bedroom, the door of which was partly open. The instant he had stepped into the ship, Blord had been aware of subtle noises. The sounds were here, too, great engines whispering in their theoretically soundproofed tubes. The primitive noises they made were dimmed by an awful suppression, yet they were unmistakably there. In this part of space, that vague rustle was a reality as sweet as life. Atomic engines working in the dead zones of Lorelei the dark.

Blord sat down in the chair the captain indicated. He wasted no time. His original purpose in coming to the destroyer star had been to get aboard the salvage ship on the scene, *this very ship,* and then use the great basic force of bribery and corruption to gain the information he must have. He wanted to know definitely whether or not Squire and Blakely were behind the piracy. He wanted the names of other salvage ships, the names of their captains, and, if possible, a list of saboteur mechanics. Also, he hoped to find a clue to the secret of the Lorelei zone engine.

Grierson did not prove difficult. Globules of sweat broke out on his heavy face after Blord offered him personally eleven million stellors. "Man," he said huskily, "I'm game. I know that this Lorelei racket won't last another year. If you can think of something—but you know that kind of animal out there." He waved his arm vaguely in the direction of the crew quarters.

"First of all," said Blord, "get the ship out of the Lorelei zone."

That too, was easy. And the problem of who would do the arguing with the crew was solved with equal simplicity. The captain saw himself receiving eleven million stellors, a sum he couldn't have made in a lifetime of Lorelei piracy. To the men Grierson made Blord's offer of a hundred thousand stellors for each individual, the money to be paid in space under conditions that would insure safety to each individual.

Blord stood in the doorway and watched the scene, fascinated. He had dealt with rough men in his time, but they had been engaged in honest work, and the roughness was merely a part of their characters. The ruling element here was fear, the atmosphere charged with latent violence.

No explanations seemed satisfactory, but the hulking commander was a determined salesman. Over and over, he described Blord's reputation for fairness. He shouted down interruptions with such ferocity that, momentarily, the men were cowed. Twice, he threw chairs at men who catcalled. At times the pandemonium was so great that no individual voice was audible. But when a measure of silence finally fell, there was the bullfrog voice of the captain, bellowing the loudest of his crew.

None of the arguments availed. Their suspicion was too great. The offer of huge sums of money was meaningless to men who distrusted their own ability to judge whether or not an idea had loopholes in it. Death, they could grasp. Dead men didn't sit in witness chairs, and identify pirates.

The end of the argument came when one of the men shouted, "He's taking up with Blord. Let's kick him out into space, too."

Grierson didn't hesitate. He plunged at the speaker, and launched his fist. The man went down with a crash, to receive a kick in the face that broke his skull. He groaned, and was dead. Grierson's voice was enormous in the startled silence.

"All right, you morons! I'm through arguing. I had to tell you about the offer, and I'm going to give you an hour to think it over. Whatever you decide at the end of that hour

129

goes. And if anyone makes so much as one objection to tha
I'll bash his face in. Now take this carrion out, and get!"

They filed almost meekly down the corridor. There was n
question that Captain Grierson had a way with his crew. Th
big man sank wearily into a chair. "Eleven million stellors,
he groaned. "The lunkheads." He looked up. "You realize, o
course, there's nothing more I can do."

"Oh, yes there is," said Blord. "And I'll guarantee you
million stellors for it, whether I live or die." He waite
tense, and saw a gleam come into the other's pale eye
Grierson said, "How would you work it?"

"Let me," Blord urged, "talk to Magrusson on the eldo. H
doesn't know the fix I'm in. You can listen and judge fro
what he says. I'll tell him to pay it to you provided you giv
me what I want first."

There was silence. The commander scowled at the floo
He said, finally, "How do you know I won't take it awa
from you the moment the call is over. And get the millio
anyway."

"Because," said Blord, "I'll pay you the other ten million
I come out of this mess alive."

There was silence once more, then, "What do you want m
to give you?"

Blord told him.

Half an hour later, Blord walked firmly to an air lock. Th
outer entrance was white with frost around the edges. Th
bitter cold chilled his thinly clad body. He watched anxious
as the lock opened. There was a hiss of escaping air. Blor
did not hesitate. He had no desire to be shot as had Professo
King. Before the two men in the spacesuits could shove hi
he leaped out. The empty blackness of space engulfed hi
instantly.

Chapter 26

Evana Travis walked to work as usual on the sixth day of her employment with Squire and Blakely. "Here I am," she thought, "secretary to Artur Blord, and I've learned enough about his methods to solve a problem for which he hasn't yet found a solution."

She had phoned Magrusson the day before and discovered that Blord was still in space. It was that that had decided her. Today must be her last day with Squire and Blakely. This morning she would finish her work against them and be back in the Blord Building before Blord returned. She laughed happily, and knew she was wonderful. "The trouble with Artur," she thought, "is that he didn't draw all the possible lessons from the crook, Corbett. He used him for a physical purpose, whereas he could have been far more valuable in other ways."

She spent the morning as she had planned, and she was just picking up her purse to leave the laboratory when the door opened and Andrew Squire and Walter Blakely came in. The junior partner smiled his mask of a smile.

"How are things?" he said.

There was something in their attitude that made her suddenly uneasy. She mustered a smile. "A few more days," she said. "I've already made several improvements that reduce the time of saturation, but I want perfection."

"Let me see one of the gadgets," Blakely said.

She handed it over. He put it in his pocket and stood staring at her. Squire, standing a few feet away, took a blaster from his pocket. He looked at Blakely, as if waiting for orders. There was no question that he was the lackey and

Blakely the master. The big man seemed unarmed. He was smoking a cigar, half leaning against one of the metal benches. His sleepy eyes were contented looking, at peace with the world.

Evana watched them tensely, wondering if they had found out what she had done. At last, she faltered, "I don't think I understand."

It was Blakely who spoke. "She doesn't understand, Mr. Squire," he said. His voice was heavy with sarcasm.

Squire did not turn his head. His eyes were like gimlets, boring into one spot, watching only her.

"It's really simple," Blakely went on. "We are about to be arrested for piracy. It will take a few years and a lot of money to fight the charge. And so we can't take any chances of the healthograph getting out of our control. In my opinion, once people can use the thing to check the state of their nutrition, it should make a billion stellors."

The Co-ordination Department of the Artur Blord Holding Company had estimated an even higher potential return.

Blakely was bracing himself, suddenly nervous. Without taking his eyes off her, he said sharply, "All right, Squire—shoot!"

Blord made one mistake. As he jumped, he used the edge of the lock for the final thrust. The cold of the metal struck through his shoe and seared the bottom of his foot, right through that immeasurably thin, flexible spacesuit underneath. Even as he fumbled hurriedly at the headpiece, with its small insert tube for oxygen capsules, and slipped a capsule into it from the supply he carried in his belt, he felt the numbness of that brief contact with metal that had been long exposed to the absolute zero of space.

There was no other hardship, no pain, nothing but darkness and waiting. The oxygen capsule, super-compressed, opened up slowly. He breathed without effort, and each capsule lasted about twenty minutes. The frozen sole of his shoe warmed gradually by induction, and there was no real cold after that. For space is not cold. Cold is contact. Cold is ice and snow and the air that touches you. These things can be cold, and can transfer cold to organic bodies.

But space *is* an absence of heat. In that perfect vacuum, a warm object gradually loses its innate heat by radiation. But so slowly that, after three hours, Blord noticed only that he was not quite so warm as he had been. There was a faint suggestion of cold to come. But at the end of three and a half hours, the energy detector capsule, for which—along with an opportunity to slip on the headgear of the special spacesuit—he had given Grierson one million stellors, produced results. A half dozen ships flashed up, and he was taken aboard the flagship of Commander Jasper, safe.

It was nearly a month later that Magrusson hurried into Blord's penthouse office on Delfi II. He was white-faced and agitated. "Artur," he said, "Hedgerow, the Companies Commissioner has just contacted me from Fasser IV. He wants to talk to you." As Blord looked up at him calmly, the general manager's agitation grew. "Don't you understand?" he exclaimed. "This is the governmental authority who can impound all your property if Squire and Blakely can prove that it was you who ruined them."

Blord said coolly, "Put him on."

It was a well-fed face that came onto the eldoplate, and the voice was smooth and baritone. After listening to him for a minute, Blord cut in:

"This is a new one on me. I didn't even know firms could be ruined these days. I thought they were protected from every kind of pressure, and even from insanity. How was it done?"

"Like every other firm," said the Commissioner, "Squire and Blakely have employees who are empowered to purchase equipment. There's a certain amount of graft always going on, but—"

Blord thought of a man named Corbett, and he smiled grimly. "Fortunately," he said, "these chaps always chisel on petty levels."

The Commissioner's smile was without humor. "Squire and

Blakely," he said, "were not that lucky. One of their women buyers ordered a hundred million stellors worth of equipment in their name, through the registered circuit. The equipment is obsolete, without resale value. And the firm is bankrupt."

"If it was a woman," said Blord, "how do I fit in?"

"Mr. Blord," the Commissioner's smile was twisted, "your most recent exploit has received wide publicity. What hasn't been so well publicized is the fact that Grierson, captain of the salvage ship, has disappeared as mysteriously as has Leah Carroll, the woman buyer. But some of the crew members turned State's evidence, and accused Squire and Blakely. Had the two men retained their wealth, the case might have been prolonged for years. As it is, from their death cell, they have appealed to the Companies Commissioner."

His twisted smile faded. He said seriously, "There's one thing I'd like to ask you, Mr. Blord. Squire and Blakely claim that they had this girl covered with a gun, and yet suddenly they woke up and realized they'd been unconscious for eighteen hours. What I'd like to know is, how could she have done that?"

"Now there," said Blord heartily, "I can help you out. I have many defenses against such unexpected threats. If I had been in this Leah Carroll's place, I would have used a gas that squirts out of a button under great pressure when the arm is raised in a certain manner, as if to ward off a blow. The effect is instantaneous."

Hedgerow laughed with genuine admiration. "Blord," he said, "congratulations on one of the smoothest performances that I have ever seen. As you know, convicted criminals cannot use the prosecuting facilities of the government, so even if we had the evidence that an agent of yours was responsible, we couldn't go after you."

The civil service executive nodded half to himself, a respectful expression on his face. He was smiling as his image faded, a knowing smile, astonishing to see on such a conservative individual.

Blord turned away from the Eldo and saw that Magrusson was wiping his face with a handkerchief. "Just suppose," he

134

mumbled, "that Squire and Blakely *hadn't* been under sentence of execution?" He shivered. "Artur," he groaned, "Evana is going to be the death of me yet. If she goes off on a tangent like this again—"

He paused, and scowled at Blord. "I can see by the look on your face that you actually approve of what she did."

Blord was smiling. "You're right," he said. "She's proved that she can handle herself under Ridge Star conditions. It's been interesting to watch her develop; but she's my kind of a woman when she can do what she did." He climbed to his feet. "I think I'll go in and tell her so."

Chapter 27

"Space preserve me," said Artur Blord, "from any more relatives like this."

He stood at the side of the bed gazing down at the unconscious body of a man about forty years of age. The man had thinning blond hair and an expression of crude cunning on his face that not even his present limp condition could effect. His name was Fred Gantley, and he was Blord's only living relative.

At last Blord turned away from the bed, and faced the agent who had brought Gantley to the Suderean Hotel on Delfi II.

"Who's been at him, Lodge?"

Lodge smiled, "Evidently, about every operator in the Ridge Stars." He began to name them.

Blord listened thoughtfully. The coming of his cousin to the Ridge Stars from far-off Earth meant little to him who had never met the man. Besides, what he had heard of

Gantley suggested that the other planned to capitalize on the Blord relationship.

As Lodge finished, giving the list of names, Blord nodded, and said cautiously, "I think they were just playing a long shot. I want to know, though, how far they were prepared to go."

Lodge said, "Going to investigate him here in the hotel?"

"Yes," said Blord.

He did not trouble to explain that the hotel was one of his properties, and that his word was law in its confines. He did add, however:

"Marian Clarke and her assistants are busy right now in the other room going over his baggage. As soon as they finish there, they'll take images of recent events from my cousin's alleged brain."

Lodge laughed. "That really ought to be worth seeing. However, it's a pleasure I'll pass up in favor of some sleep. Call me if you need me, chief." He went out.

An hour later, Blord stood whistling softly under his breath. "Twenty-eight people!" he said. He shook his head wonderingly, then he shrugged. "Well, what else have we got?"

Marian Clarke was calm. "He was given five suits," she said, "each one of which had electronic devices woven into them. Altogether, there were nine listening devices, and three methods of transmitting the images of every one in his vicinity. But now," she went on briskly, "if you'll sit down we'll do a quick run-over of the things he remembers and also of what he doesn't consciously remember while various people had him under their influence."

The pictures that showed on the screen varied in brightness and interest, but at such moments as these it was hard to bore Artur Blord. He had prospered in the Ridge Stars because he anticipated dangers, and because he was alert to unexpected developments. He had no idea what he was looking for, and he did not recognize it immediately even when it came. The scene that really interested him was several moments past when he realized it.

He waved at Marian and said, "Those little animals back

there—let's have another look at them." He gazed with alert eyes at the tiny horned things as they flashed again on the screen, and then sat frowning, but still intent, while the rest of the pictures were shown.

Afterward, while the helpers were gathering up their equipment preparatory to leaving the suite, Marian Clarke came over to Blord. "What made you stop the screen at those tiny beasts?" she asked.

"Ever see their kind before?" asked Blord.

She shrugged. "There are so many animals on the inhabited planets," she said. "No one can possibly keep track of them. Where did you see them before?"

"I saw drawings of them," Blord said slowly, "paintings of them on the walls of buildings that no longer exist."

Marian stared at him, her eyes widening. "So did I," she breathed. Her eyes gleamed. "But I thought the Skal had left this part of the galaxy after you destroyed his castle."

The man and woman gazed at each other, their eyes thoughtful. Marian spoke again, "But why was your cousin shown the animals? Is this a trap? Besides, why would the Skal take the risk of having animals like that shipped to it? Where did they come from? And what are they used for?"

Blord laughed. "Stop popping questions at me like that. I can't answer any of them."

He fell silent. The Skal was no laughing matter. Remorseless, cunning, possessed of scientific secrets unknown to human beings, the Skal had escaped the destruction of his castle without, apparently, ever having been personally in danger. It was a point that Blord had never forgotten.

Blord shook the recollection from his mind, and said slowly, "One thing we didn't find out is what stimulated my cousin into making the trip out here. It seems hard to believe that he hoped to obtain money from me—after all these years ..."

In the corner of the room, the eldophone tinkled softly. As Blord walked toward it, a plump face appeared on it. The face was white and anxious, and the man's voice, when he spoke, was a high-pitched squeak: "It's outrageous, Artur—it's highway robbery, that's what it is. It's—"

Blord bent over the eldophone. "Control yourself, Magrusson." He spoke sharply, despite the fact that he was accustomed to the dramatic reactions of his business manager.

Magrusson's agitation grew. "But you don't understand, Artur!" he exclaimed. "They're the legal government of the Ridge Stars, and they can—" He broke off, made a visible effort at self-control, and said finally with a semblance of calm, "You'd better talk to the man yourself. He'll explain it better than I can.

It was a youngish, arrogant face that came onto the eldoplate. The broad shoulders were clothed in the dark blue of the Ridge Star Patrol. The arrogance was also in his voice as the officer said, "You are Artur Blord, of the Artur Blord Holding Company, Limited?"

Blord studied the patrol officer curiously. The man was a stranger to him, but such a stiff, hostile attitude in a member of the patrol's head office was unusual. He had long considered the patrol commissioner, Lane Stetson, a good friend. There was no friendliness in the face that looked at him boldly from the eldoplate now.

Blord said at last, mildly, "I am Artur Blord."

The man said, "I have been commissioned to inform you that as of today, a twenty-five per cent levy will be made on interplanetary transactions of the Artur Blord Holding Company, Limited. All moneys are to be sent to patrol headquarters on Marmora II the first of each month. You will be formally notified. That is all."

Blord blinked. "Just a minute! What—"

Magrusson groaned, "Twenty-five per cent, Artur. It's fantastic. We're ruined!"

"Magrusson!" Blord said sharply, and the plump man subsided. "Young man," Blord said to the patrol officer, "this is a new one on me. I'll have to ask you to explain further. The patrol is not empowered to levy taxes. They are strictly a law-enforcing organization operating in the Ridge Stars."

The young officer was cold. "We have received proper

authorization," he said. "Our reason is that piracy is on the increase. Operators who are the direct beneficiaries of our new, larger service must pay the cost—a twenty-five percent tax. Recalcitrants will not receive the protection of the patrol." He shrugged again, and the arrogance was strong in his voice. "We'll expect your initial payment on the first of the month." There was a sharp click, and his face was gone from the eldoplate.

Blord sat for several seconds, scowling, and then he stared satirically at the quivering Magrusson. Finally he turned, and looked long and searchingly at the unconscious body of Fred Gantley. He said half to himself, "It seems impossible that there could be any connection but—"

He turned to the plump man, whose image was still on the eldoplate. "Magrusson, I'm going to call Lane Stetson, the patrol commissioner, and find out what's going on. We have no objection to paying a legitimate tax, but I know the piracy situation as well as they do; and it doesn't justify such extreme action. Space is too big, pirate ships can just fade into the distance, and there are countless hiding places. There's a point at which extra money spent on the police brings no return. You listen in, will you?"

Magrusson's face faded from the plate. Blord made some adjustments on the eldo instrument board. And then, the face of a uniformed switchboard operator came onto the plate.

"I'm sorry," said the man, after he had listened to Blord's request, "Mr. Lane Stetson is no longer with the Patrol; and Jason Gregory, the new commissioner, is not accepting outside calls for the time being."

"Where is Stetson?" Blord asked.

"I'm sorry—" Formally—"I'm not permitted to give any further information."

The man's face blurred, and disappeared. Magrusson came back onto the plate. Blord was frowning. Finally, slowly, he said: "Magrusson, there's something up. I'm going to Marmora II. I'll report to you later—what's the matter."

"Uh, Artur," he said unhappily, "I hate to bother you with

small matters at a time like this, but you'll be gone several weeks and—what about the ghost?"

Blord groaned, "That's all I need—a haunted warehouse!" He broke off curtly, "You'll have to take care of that yourself, Magrusson. I can't take the time now."

Magrusson persisted. "I tell you, Artur, so many men are quitting that it's—after all, you said you'd go down and investigate!"

Blord said impatiently, "Tell them to stop acting like children."

He clicked off the machine, and turned to Marian. "Look after him, will you Marian," he said, nodding at Gantley. He went out without another word.

Chapter 28

Brian Emerson turned away from the eldo-receiver which, for the past hour, had been tuned in to the suit Gantley was wearing. He rubbed his hands together in satisfaction.

"A smooth performance, Ashleyton," he said. "He's coming right into our trap." He stood up, a big, saturnine-looking man of fifty-five. The smile on his face accentuated rather than diminished the aura of intellectual and physical strength that radiated from him. "Ashleyton, going after a man like Blord provides the kind of intellectual pleasure that makes life worth living for me. And this time I feel sure that he hasn't got a chance. The idea of bringing his cousin here was a stroke of genius."

Ashleyton said, "I'm going to be interested in that Coordination Department of his."

Emerson nodded with satisfaction. "All of us have some

special interest in Blord. We'll take him apart, and see what makes him tick."

Ashleyton was frowning. "What about this reference to a ghost at the end of their discussion?"

Emerson waved an impatient arm. "Why bother about the neuroses of a warehouse worker?" He smiled sardonically, and there was exultation in his voice. "The best part of all this is that Blord is no more than a side issue, a tidbit to be swallowed in the biggest gobbling-up process ever conceived in the mind of one man. I'd like to see his face when it begins to dawn on him that I've taken over the entire government of the Ridge Stars."

Two weeks and five days went by.

For Emerson, at Patrol Headquarters, they had been vital days for his plan. Hour after hour, night and day, coded messages arrived telling how one man had been killed, another replaced, a third cowed into submission. In thousands of government officers, on more than two hundred planets, his agents were at work seizing key positions in the Ridge Star Government by murder, pressure, persuasion and bribery.

He kept himself awake with drugs. When he slept, it was for fifteen minutes or half an hour. Even his enormous energy began to flag. He thought of Blord suddenly, one morning, looked at the date on his desk chronometer, felt amazed, and angrily rang for Ashleyton. While he waited, he climbed to his feet and walked to the window. It was a transparent plastic glass nearly fifty feet wide, and it looked out on a scene that still fascinated him though he had seen it daily now for more than a month.

The planet Marmora II had been selected originally by Earth Government Space Patrol as an ideal site for a Space Patrol base. The planet was as close to its parent body as Mercury was to Sol. It turned the same face forever to its sun, and the day side was a blasted, burning hell; the night side an icy, frozen waste where the temperature hovered close to absolute zero. Airless, its surface torn by past convulsions, its face seamed and old, it wheeled around its sun rocking slightly in its orbit.

The eccentricity was small. Over a period of about twenty-eight sidereal hours, the planet wobbled through a pattern. The slight variation created a narrow ribbon of alternating light and dark, where the eternal, blistering day met the frozen, everlasting night. For fourteen hours that purgatorial area sweltered in the daytime heat, and then as the planet rolled in its course, it shifted over into the frosty darkness.

There, in that nightmare facsimile of Earth's gentle night and day period, the Ridge Star Space Patrol had its headquarters. With its buildings, its shops, its landing fields and its residential sections, it occupied a space of some four hundred square miles, and it was covered from one end to the other by a series of domes.

Emerson gazed out from his high, centrally located office across glass-smooth miles of transparent plastic—the top of the dome. In that airless reach, distances were startlingly deceptive. The black sky, with its stars, seemed just beyond his window. The mountainous landscape, which began at the very edge of the dome, though many miles away, stood out so sharply that he had the impression that he could see even the smallest objects.

He was still standing there when Ashleyton, answering his call, came in.

Without speaking, the instrument wizard went to Emerson's desk and laid down a manuscript. The great man walked over, picked it up and read the first page with a stormy frown that became a thundercloud of anger. He pounded the desk with his fist.

"What's the matter with you?" he raged. "Blord should have been here a week ago. Where is he? What's he up to? What made him suspicious?"

Ashleyton shrugged. Though as tall as Emerson, he lacked the other's weight and build. But he was used to the great man's furies. He said coldly, "Maybe he changed his mind. After all, he did try to get in touch with Stetson. When that failed—"

Emerson's anger subsided as quickly as it had come. His expression grew thoughtful. He said slowly, "That would

142

merely make him cautious. In his place, if I were to discover that Stetson had had a fatal accident, I would try to find out what had happened. Is there any record at all of significant activity in the Blord Holding Company?"

Ashleyton indicated the report. "You didn't go beyond page one."

Emerson returned his attention to the document. Presently, he shook his head admiringly. "Ashleyton, I've got to admit it. Blord is quick. Even as he was speeding through space, he was negotiating with the spacemen's union, and in return for higher wages they've agreed to fly his ships whether they get Space Patrol protection or not. He hasn't actually refused to pay the tax, but has secured a court injunction while he fights the tax in the courts. Simultaneously, his organization is starting a vast political campaign to throw out of office the delegates who authorized the tax. And that's just a small part. So far, he's anticipated our every move except one. And I wouldn't be surprised if in the back of his mind he isn't considering even that possibility. The amazing part is that he's done it all without even knowing that we're in the game. Ashleyton, we've got to find out if he's here, working against us under our very noses."

He had seated himself; now, restlessly, he climbed to his feet, and walked to the window. He motioned jerkily to the desolate splendor of the scene beyond it. He said, "How would you penetrate Patrol Headquarters? And what would you do to catch someone who did penetrate it in disguise?"

They discussed the problem at some length. Emerson said finally, grimly, "He may be able to disguise himself effectively, but he can't alter his size and build. We've got to trace him down. As soon as we've narrowed our list of suspects to four or five, we'll start killing them one by one. Get the others to help you. I regard this of the utmost importance."

He paused; then said earnestly, "Artur Blord wrecked our plans once before. We've got to make sure that he doesn't do it again. The best method is to kill him. The alternative is to destroy his organization so completely that he becomes just another little man without resources.

"And—" He smiled grimly—"we're in the position where we can do either, or both."

Chapter 29

During the next five days, Emerson had several thoughts about Blord. Each time, he took immediate action. His first plan involved going up in a space ship and coming down like any new arrival.

When he had originally come to the base, as Jason Gregory, the new commissioner, he hadn't paid too much attention to the landing. Now, he watched every detail. He had previously advised the control tower of his intention. As he approached, he eldophoned his identity, and then he stood by, waiting for permission to come down.

Ships were coming in and going out almost every minute. Entry and exit was accomplished through scores of airlocks in the plastic dome. All around his ship the sky was dotted with vessels waiting to land with freight and equipment. And every little while, a sleek patrol warship slid along one or the other of three special lanes, and all intermediate traffic was cleared while it landed.

By the time the eldophone buzzed half an hour later, giving him permission to land, Emerson was ready to test his plan. He put his ship into a "dead" lane, and went down in a life boat. He entered the airlock to which he had been assigned, and put the small craft into a cradle; then he climbed out and took a surface car for Patrol City.

No one interfered with him. No one questioned his action in landing a lifeboat instead of a ship. Nor did anyone during the next few days notify him that his lifeboat had overstayed its time.

On the strength of the test, Emerson inquired as to how many cradles had been in use for a week or more. The answer was significant. Not counting those used by the Patrol itself, there were 194. All of them were large ships; there were no small craft. Baffled, Emerson inquired what precautions were taken to prevent Patrol cradles from being used illegally. He was told that the regulations forbade outsiders the use of Patrol cradles. Emerson restrained himself with difficulty.

"So much for the regulations," he said steadily to the officer who had given him the information. "What do you actually *do* to prevent illegal use of them?"

The officer whose image was on the eldo-local plate was quite unflustered. "We keep a record," he said. "We check the cradles periodically."

"How often?" sharply.

"There's no fixed time. We try to keep it random." For the first time, the man seemed to become aware of Emerson's exasperation. He added hastily, "It's about a month since the last one was made—would you like another one?"

"Yes," said Emerson softly. And broke the connection.

He was duly informed that an unauthorized lifeboat had been discovered as a result of the check-up. The officer expressed himself as astounded. "It's never happened before," he said.

Emerson said coldly, "How would you know?" He went on without waiting for a reply, "I want a system developed to prevent such unauthorized use of a cradle in the future." He broke off, "Does the lifeboat have any identifying marks?"

"None."

"Did you check its registration?"

"It was manufactured illegally."

Emerson nodded, half to himself. There were many such craft. Space was too big to keep track of hidden factories. His own organization had purchased ships of every size and description, including duplicates of Patrol warships. Though it was illegal, there was not an operator in the Ridge Stars who did not find occasional need for an unregistered craft. It was not surprising that Blord had casually taken the risks involved. The discovery of Blord's lifeboat—he was certain of the identification—exhilarated him. He gave final instructions: "Leave the boat where it is. I'll come out and have a look at it myself. That's all."

The officer's face vanished from the plate.

Emerson expected to find no clues on his visit to the lifeboat; and he found none. Before leaving the craft, however, he had a mechanic from his own organization build in a governor which would cut off the power when the boat had climbed four hundred feet. A fall from that height was enough to kill a man.

On his way back to his office, he thoughtfully paused at the public transport sheds and inquired in minute detail into the workings of the organization. His informant was a short, stocky, bettle-browed man who had a habit of shrugging when he spoke.

He said importantly, "We handled 98,000 passengers for the outside last year." He shrugged. "Many people do not want to pay the high cradle rental—and of course there are those who come in commercial liners."

Emerson asked, "When you take people down from or up to their ships, is there any special procedure you have to go through? Do you have to report to anybody? Does the individual have to be identified?"

The other shrugged. "Our system is better than that. Every passenger's face and name is flashed to the control tower. If he has been posted, we get a coded signal and there's a Patrol officer waiting in the airlock to pick him up."

Back in his office, Emerson had Blord "posted," and as an additional precaution had a number of Ashleyton's structure machines built in to every entrance of the Public Transport Building and at the various airlocks. Other protective devices were being installed, he knew, but so far there hadn't been time to do the perfect job of which Ashleyton and his technicians were capable.

As a final precaution, he checked the methods by which outsiders registered at hotels, or stayed at the homes of patrol employees, or went via groundside airlocks out onto the hostile planet itself.

He was still tightening the loopholes he found when Ashleyton came again to see him. Ashleyton announced somberly: "I've come for help. Murrison and I can't handle the situation."

Emerson gazed at him, lips pursed. He had been thinking that the situation was very much in hand and Ashleyton's remark momentarily unsettled him. He recovered swiftly. After all, he reflected, none of the others knew what he had been doing. He said slowly, feeling the need for a clear picture:

"Murrison worked with you?"

Ashleyton nodded. "The others were busy. But you know Murrison—never too busy to kill somebody."

Emerson smiled grimly. Murrison was the greatest living authority on nuclear physics, but he had a number of exciting hobbies, among them murder in its more refined forms. It was Murrison who had prepared the generalized structure of the Ridge Star government on the basis of which key men were being murdered or otherwise eliminated. If Murrison and Ashleyton, working together, had run into trouble, it was time for Brian Emerson personally to take a hand. He said sharply:

"How do you mean—help?"

Ashleyton was intent. "We've narrowed the search down to three men. If one of the three isn't Blord then he's not here at Patrol Headquarters."

"That's a broad statement. There are more than 80,000 men here."

The other said earnestly, "We used teams of men, with every available measuring instrument and after all, we do have a physical record of Blord from the last—"

He stopped discreetly, evidently not wanting to arouse unpleasant memories. Emerson said curtly, "Go on. You have his measurements. Did you test every adult?"

"Even those in the hospitals."

"And you narrowed it down to three?" Emerson scowled. "Why didn't you kill them and see what happened?"

"I'm coming to that." Ashleyton ran his fingers distractedly through his thinning hair. "You know Murrison. He believes in statistical methods."

Emerson waited grimly. He knew Murrison very well indeed. The physicist gave the most loving care and attention to his hobby. Ashleyton went on:

"He thought up three methods of causing accidental death. We used a different one on each of the three suspects. When they failed, we switched them around, until all three methods had been tried on each man." Ashleyton shook his head uneasily. "Chief, Murrison swears that the chances against all of them failing are about a million to one. So far, we've done nothing openly. What do you suggest?"

Emerson's mind had been made up for several seconds. "Have them brought in to me. I'll guarantee to recognize Blord in just about three seconds, regardless of his disguise."

They came in as a group, and they seemed puzzled that the new commissioner wanted to see them. Emerson shook hands with each in turn, thoughtfully, wondering if there might not be some subtle difference in the way Blord would grasp his hand. If there was, he could not detect it.

He sat down, baffled but still confident. He glanced at Murrison, who had come in with the men. The physicist was the youngest of the renegade scientists who had followed him out into space. He was just over five feet eleven, and slim of build. He looked tired now, which was not surprising. Like the others, he had been working night and day. His voice, when he spoke, was hoarse:

"Mr. Gregory—" He used Emerson's pseudonym politely and apparently without having to think about it—"I think you should turn these gentlemen directly over to me. I have in mind taking them on a short exploratory trip."

One of the three men spoke up briskly. "Mr. Gregory," he said, "we're all a little puzzled by your action in sending for us. Naturally, we're all anxious to please the new commissioner, and—"

Emerson cut him off, saying to Murrison, "Have you any preference among these gentlemen?" He meant: "Which one of the three do you think is Blord?"

Murrison shook his head. "Not at the moment."

"I see," said Emerson. "So it will be necessary to take all three on the trip."

Once again, Murrison nodded. He said, "We might have a final discussion on the matter once we're out in space. At that point we can be very frank with each other."

For a moment, Emerson was amused. He could imagine the nature of the frankness. The men would be stripped, and their disguises penetrated. He did not doubt that the job would be a thorough one. He couldn't help but agree that it was the best method. It was dangerous to kill men within the confines of Patrol City. The number of accidental deaths that had already taken place made even that method unwise for the moment, but out in space in a ship manned by members of his own organization, murder would be easy.

It was five days later when Ashleyton burst in upon him, and gasped:

"We've just found Murrison's body."

Emerson looked blank, then his mind reached out and grasped the implication.

"You mean, the fellow who brought those three men here—who took them out into space—that was Blord pretending to be Murrison—"

He settled back in his chair, fighting for self control. He said finally, softly, half to himself, "All right, Mr. Blord, let's see what you can do against the power of the Ridge Star Government."

He leaned over, and clicked on the eldophone. His eyes were narrowed, his face grim. As soon as he had his connection, he began to issue orders.

Chapter 30

In escaping Patrol Headquarters, Artur Blord felt gloomy rather than exultant. The ability to disguise himself as Murrison, Emerson's henchman, was an achievement he took more or less for granted. In entering the patrol city, he had had for a short time the advantage of secrecy.

It was that that had saved him. The identification of the Emerson gang as the organization that had taken over the Patrol had been a complete surprise. Realizing immediately how great his own danger was, he had stalked and killed Murrison because that cold-blooded individual was the nearest to his own build of the men who comprised the inner core of the gang.

And so he had escaped. So much sustained, sleepless effort, so many precautions merely to get away—it emphasized the extent of Emerson's success.

From this moment on, Artur Blord was a marked man. He could be killed; and the vast authority of the Patrol could be used to make it appear like an accident. And that was true even if it happened before witnesses on a city street.

From this moment on, he had none of the protections of an ordinary citizen.

The Emerson ship had barely left the airlock of Patrol Headquarters before Artur Blord headed for the nearest escape hatch. In his guise of Murrison, commander of the vessel, no one questioned his movements. It was doubtful if any member of the crew even noticed the departure of a lifeboat.

Blord reached his own yacht in its lane high above the

planet. He set course for the Delfi sun, put the ship into automatic flight, and went to bed.

When he awakened, he had a plan.

It would be unwise to try to handle Emerson alone. For once, he needed the support of other Ridge Star operators. He headed for the control board, frowning over the difficulties. The great business operators whom he knew were not noted for their willingness to cooperate. Even where their own interests were involved, they had been known to prefer to work alone.

The question was, where was he in space? Who could he talk to most easily?

Sitting in the control chair, Blord studied his instruments. The one hundred and ninety-four Ridge Star suns spread in an uneven line over a distance of about two hundred light years. Seen from a certain angle, they actually gave the impression of being a bright ridge in the darkness. They had been named in orderly fashion, beginning with the letter A and running progressively up to Z.

He discovered that he was passing the "I" suns, Izcudun, Imogene, and Idyllic. Since he was coming from Marmora and heading toward Delfi, he was going "down the line."

Without looking it up, Blord knew that the "I" suns had five habitable planets among them. They were all on a comparatively primitive level, the operators being of small importance in the Ridge Star scheme of things, though one at least controlled his planet. The largest city had a population of just over a million, and it had been built principally with Blord money—though most of the inhabitants didn't know that.

Blord continued on his course. He was already looking ahead, and considering the Hargan sun—the great "H" as it was called. There he would find Hargan's planet and Hargan's city. And, if he paused, he would presently find himself face to face with Geoffrey Hargan himself.

Thinking about Hargan in itself gave Blord pause. And yet, who could be better for his purposes? If he could win Hargan to his viewpoint, several other operators would fall in line.

Despite the rationalization, Blord approached the Hargan sun indecisively. As he drew near Hargan's planet, he considered the alternatives. Should he be satisfied with an eldophone conversation with the man, or risk a personal interview?

The dangerous potentiality of the latter course made him hesitate, but finally it seemed to him that he had no recourse. Many times he had noticed that an eldo conversation between two people, each sitting in his own office, did not have the impact of a personal meeting.

The great Hargan would sit up and take notice if Artur Blord came down into his stronghold, and apparently placed himself in the power of a rival.

Lips pressed into a thin line, eyes narrowed as he thought of the protective measures he would have to take, Artur Blord decided nevertheless to take the chance.

As the shadow of night lengthened over the planet, Blord launched a lifeboat and landed it by remote control at one of his secret properties near Hargan's city.

Then he put his yacht in an orbit around the planet, advised Hargan of his coming, and went down in a second lifeboat.

He was arrested as he stepped out of his lifeboat, and taken immediately to Hargan's building, which was located in the very center of the city.

He found himself presently under guard in a large, comfortably furnished library. Though he had never been in the room before, Blord guessed grimly that this was Hargan's private study.

Behind Blord, a door opened. Blord turned. A tall, powerful looking man stood in the doorway. His intelligent face was set in an insolent expression. He was somewhat heavier than Emerson; his head was bigger, and he had the suggestion of a paunch, whereas Emerson merely looked big and strong. But the over-all physical resemblance between the two men was remarkable.

Hargan settled himself in a chair near the door. "Artur," he said in a hearty voice, "this is a pleasant surprise."

Blord held up his handcuffed hands. "Jeff," he said, "surely you're not going to leave these on me." It was one of the ironic usages that the top operators in the Ridge Stars addressed each other by their first names, just as if they were friends.

Hargan frowned. "Artur," he said, "the fact is, you're a dangerous man. Nobody knows just how you work, but there are mysterious accounts of what you can do. For all I know you've come to assassinate me. Tell me, what's on your mind?"

Swiftly, Blord described the background of the new tax. He finished quietly, "So you see what we're up against. A group of scientists who have more know-how than anything either Earth or the Ridge Stars can muster. And they've already gained control of our police force."

There was silence after Blord had finished. He had the impression that Hargan was puzzled. The man said abruptly:

"Am I to understand that you feel Emerson has done something he ought not to?"

Blord stared at him in amazement. Then he said, "We seem to be having communication difficulties. Am *I* to understand that Emerson's seizure of control doesn't trouble you?"

Hargan shrugged. "A new operator in the field. Seems to be quite an ambitious person. If he gets in my way, I'll slap him down."

Blord leaned back in his chair. The first shock was over, but the surprise continued. It was not that he hadn't run into this attitude before. Many Ridge Star operators were so amoral that only with the greatest difficulty were they kept within bounds. But he had expected that Hargan would be able to distinguish between an operator who accepted certain rules and regulations, and a criminal who didn't.

Blord said finally, "He's not only in your way already, but he's going to be conducting his affairs at your expense. Just wait till the Patrol starts collecting a twenty-five per cent tax on all your transactions."

Hargan was cool. "I'm astonished to see you so excited. Why not be like me? Take it calmly. Sure, they've got a tax—on paper. But men have to collect it. On Hargan's planet, the collectors are *my* men—or they will be if they know what's good for them.

"You see—" his tone grew confidential; he seemed unconcerned that half a dozen guards stood by—"you played this game all wrong, Artur. You're just an operator. Sure, you can bribe politicians. You can influence laws to some extent. On Hargan's planet, I make the laws. I control the cities, the police. I'm an operator, yes. Perhaps, I'm not so well known as you are. Possibly, your activities are on a wider scale. I estimate that you actually possess about twice as much money and property as I do, perhaps even three times as much.

"But here on Hargan's planet, I'm boss. Through my political power, I control more money than either you or I legally own. The entire resources of a planet are at my disposal."

He shrugged again. "So you see, Emerson doesn't mean a thing to me. If necessary, I'll make a deal with him. Naturally, the Patrol will be able to collect some tax from me. Why not? If they succeed in stopping piracy—"

Blord said, "Jeff, you're blind. Emerson *is* the pirate chief. That's what I've been trying to tell you."

Hargan blinked, and his eyes lighted. "Well, I'll be a—" He shook his head wonderingly, and then said in an admiring tone: "Artur, the man is a genius. I couldn't have done it better myself."

Chapter 31

Blord decided it was time to leave Hargan's planet. The decision did not change his situation. He leaned back in his chair to give the impression that he was prepared for a long argument. Actually, his mind was already seeking some method that would gain him a quick escape from the room.

There were, he saw in a casually quick glance, six guards watching him. The very way in which they stood was significant. Two were near his chair, presumably ready to leap on him if he made the slightest move. There was a man at each of the two doors. The remaining two, huge men both, hovered protectingly near Hargan.

Blord said slowly, "Jeff, I have an idea that you've forgotten the temporary nature of all this that you and I have achieved, and of the whole frontier-style life that we have in the Ridge Stars. Remember, it was a deliberate Earth policy to let the profit motive pace man's expansion out to the galaxy. Rampant industrial capitalism has proved itself effective many times in a fast-growing economy, but here in our area of space, it's just about run its course."

He paused, saw that again there was a puzzled expression on Hargan's face; and went on quickly:

"The original purpose of the almost unlimited license we have had to do what we pleased, has been pretty well accomplished. The public attitude toward the big operator is changing. These men here—"

He waved his manacled hands at the guards, contriving to strike the wrist of the one who stood at his left. It was a skilful, apparently aimless and spontaneous action, but it achieved an exact, desired result. He managed to dig the man with one of his rings. The needle in the ring was very short, being just long enough to penetrate the thickest skin. But it was hollow, and it injected a hynotic drug into the guard's arm.

The drug carried its own lightning-swift anesthetic. The pain of the thrust, never more than equivalent to a slight scratch, faded even as the needle entered the skin. If the guard felt the prick of the needle, he gave no indication of it. He continued to stand at attention.

Blord went on, as if he were unaware of the incident: "—these guards of yours are no longer your men in the way they were ten years ago. They won't admit it, but they've got secret reservations."

Hargan seemed to have recovered himself. He said suavely, "Any man who doesn't want to work for me can quit at any time."

He broke off impatiently: "Artur, this is the most defeatist talk I've ever heard. What amazes me is that I'm hearing it from a man who is reputed to be unbeatable. Don't you realize that what Earth planned two hundred years ago doesn't mean anything now? There are different people today. The descendants of the planners are just men, who can be bought and sold, corrupted, re-educated, as easily as the people that you and I have dealt with all these years. The truth is that there are hundreds of trillionaires out in space for every one on Earth. People didn't dream of such a thing in those idealistic days. The experiment has run wild. Nobody can control it, least of all an Earth Government which has so little to offer to the ambitious man that a great scientist like Emerson comes out here to be an operator in our fashion."

Blord hadn't intended to listen. He was trying to decide just how he would make use of the hypnotized guard. When the moment came, his control of the situation must be so complete that no violence would be necessary.

Briefly, he forgot that. Because Hargan's words *sounded* true. Blord had a flashing picture of the reality behind them, and saw that for once he had let himself think unrealistically. The great experiment *was* out of hand. All these years there had been in the back of his mind a faith that everything would work out right. Even as his own enterprises spread octopus-like over this part of the galaxy, he had envisioned a more stable society.

With a sigh, he realized now that it had been a kind of deliberate self-delusion. He had never let it influence his own actions in a crisis, and had always regarded it more as a spiritual check on the vaunting and deadly ambitions of men like Hargan than as a concrete control. Now, he saw that it actually meant nothing.

In one jump, he was back to dependence on himself. There

was no kindly grandfather watching over human affairs. Emerson could win the Ridge Stars, with all that that meant in terms of catastrophe for civilization—and for himself as an individual.

Blord began to stiffen to the tremendous fact. Just for a moment he had been afraid. He recognized that, even if he could get away from Hargan, he was in for the greatest struggle of his life. But that was the point. It was the struggle that counted, not its result.

At this moment, and at each successive moment, he would do things and say things that mattered in themselves. Each tiny action he took, each word, would change whatever situation he was in, for better or for worse.

It was the journey, not the arrival at the destination; not the experience as a whole but the moment itself—the excitement of a penetrating remark, the inescapable logic of an action taken at exactly the right instant of time: These were the realities of his life.

Beside such conditioning, such an ability to live for each second during a period of danger—power and wealth and success were as nothing. So he believed. So he acted now. He said:

"Jeff, you and I are wasting time discussing this. As you can see—" He held up his manacled hands—"I came here at considerable risk to convince you personally. By this time you must feel reasonably certain that I am not going to assassinate you, but that in fact I'm going to need your help in the future, and you—whether you believe it or not—are going to need mine. How about taking these off, and letting me go to my lifeboat?"

He waited, curious. The simplest solution for his present situation would be for Hargan to let him go. The great man shifted uncomfortably in his chair. He said slowly:

"Artur, you make me feel bad. Years ago, after a little operation of yours that cost me a billion stellors, I dreamed of a moment like this when you would be sitting in one of my offices, wearing—" He shuddered delicately—"those things—"

Blord said, "Surely, that dream derives from the childish period of your career, when you still felt insecure."

"It isn't that," Hargan said unhappily, "I find it hard to imagine you actually getting up and going out of here. I find myself reluctant—" Once more he failed to finish a sentence.

Blord realized, grimly, what the other meant. Hargan had an enemy in his control, and he was loath to let him go. Blord said frankly:

"Jeff, the alternative is murder or imprisonment."

"I know, I know." Regretfully.

"For once," said Blord, "The best method is the friendly one. I intend to fight Emerson. If I win, it's your victory also."

"Still," temporized Hargan, "your victory under the circumstances you've outlined to me is problematical. I might be better advised to contact Emerson, and find out just what he thinks of all this—" He paused, as if a great light had come. He went on, "You know, that wouldn't do any harm at all, would it?"

He broke off. "I can see it now. First, Emerson offers me a hundred million stellors for you. Then you make a bid of two hundred million if I let you go. Finally, Emerson offers to forget all about my paying the twenty-five per cent tax." He stopped. His eyes were bright and hard. "What do you think of that, Artur?"

It was a decision. Blord took one mental look at the picture, and realized that he had lost the verbal battle. Without hesitation, he acted.

He twisted toward the hypnotized guard, and pointed his hands at the man. "You!" he said in a piercing tone.

He didn't wait for a reply. Clearly, firmly, swiftly, he ordered: "Draw your gun! Step back! Cover everybody! Shoot anybody who resists!"

The surprise was complete. Hargan cursed softly in amazement, but at Blord's suggestion he ordered the handcuffs removed from Blord's wrists. He seemed resigned. "Artur," he said admiringly, "I don't know how you did that, but it's terrific."

Blord wasted no time. He disarmed the other guards, and ordered the hypnotized man to keep them at bay. Then he slipped through the door by which Hargan had earlier entered the library. He found himself in a large dressing room.

At top speed, Blord undressed. He removed his outer clothes down to a thin, very light but opaque cover-all undersuit of the kind used in space to protect the body against sudden changes in temperature. Without hesitation, he removed the undersuit.

Beneath was that most fragile of all materials, an invisibility suit.

Quickly, Blord drew the folded shoulder hood—with its fitted pair of glasses—over his head. And then, before fastening it, he called through the open door:

"Have one of the men open the door to the corridor."

No one saw him. Just for a moment, as he passed through each doorway, he must have been tenuously visible, the vaguest of shadowy figures. He kept to the center of the hallway. At the elevator shaft, he waited for a vacant machine. The attendant at the main floor must have been surprised when an elevator came down, the door opened, and no one emerged from it. He showed his surprise by going over to it, and peering inside. By that time, Blord was slipping past the police officers who guarded the main entrance.

Outside, he headed for the lifeboat he had hidden beyond the outskirts of Hargan's City.

As he climbed to his spaceship, he did not delude himself. He had failed again. Hargan's refusal to join him against Emerson was a major setback. There were other operators, of course; and he would contact them as swiftly as possible. But there would be many like Hargan. And even those who agreed to help might become lukewarm when they discovered they were in the minority.

It was even possible that he would have to fight Emerson alone.

On his way once more, he called Magrusson for the first

time. The plump man listened with pale face to Blord's account.

He himself had nothing to report.

It seemed to Blord that there was nothing he could do but continue on to Delfi, and be on hand for further developments. He said as much to Magrusson, finished:

"Keep me in touch."

He broke the connection.

Chapter 32

He was leaning back, considering his next moves, when the eldo sounded again. It was Magrusson, his eyes round with excitement.

"Artur," he gasped, "the Space Patrol has just issued a statement in connection with you. I recorded it. Listen—"

His face faded from the screen; there was a pause, and then a voice said:

"Ladies and gentlemen, Space Patrol Headquarters have issued the following special statement: 'The Ridge Star Government has authorized the seizure of the Artur Blord Holding Company as of noon today. This seizure is made necessary by Blord's arbitrary refusal to participate in the Patrol's attack against piracy, which has now become a major menace to all space traffic. The lives of thousands of men are endangered by this one operator's autocratic action, so his company's business will be conducted by the Patrol in the public interest until such time as the spaceways are again relatively safe. In order to guarantee that the interests of the owner will be looked after, the patrol is appointing Artur Blord's only living relative, Frederick Gantley, to be custodian of the property.'"

Magrusson's face came back on the screen, as the message ended. Blord stared for a moment at the pale, puffy cheeks of the other, then said softly:

"So that's why they brought my cousin here."

The general manager seemed not to hear. He said in a moaning voice:

"Artur, what are we going to do? They can ruin us. We can be sold out without our being able to say a word or raise a finger. The entire business can be disposed of before anyone finds out about it."

The possibility had already occurred to Blord. As he realized its import, he had his first conviction of disaster. Most people didn't know it, but the reputation of Artur Blord was partly an illusion. He used power and money with imagination.

That was his forte. He had never denied it to himself. With thousands of men to do his will, with millions of money to channel in any direction he pleased, miracles could be wrought. He had wrought them. True, he was clever—he didn't deny that either—and he could probably make more money. But times had changed. There were too many intrenched fortunes now, where once had been wilderness and endless opportunity. The magic success of Artur Blord would probably never again be possible.

Magrusson said, "Artur, can we trust that cousin of yours?"

Blord caught hold of himself. "Of course not," he said irritably. "Fred is just a babe in the woods. We've got to get him out of the way. Where is he? Have you got control of him?"

Magrusson groaned. "We keep an eye on him. He lives in barrooms."

"Kidnap him. Take him out somewhere until I can land and size up the situation."

He saw shrewdly that at this early stage, there would be confusion. In so great and complex an organization, no one coming into it for the first time—as were Emerson's men—could hope to trace down the tens of thousands of transactions that were occurring at any given moment. Nor could anyone hazard more than a wild guess as to the amount of money on hand at a hundred Blord-controlled banks.

Swiftly, through Evana, he called all his former secretaries out of retirement, and gave them precise instructions as to certain deposit boxes which they were entitled to visit in his name.

The action gave him a special feeling of pleasure. He had received much criticism, and publicity, over his generosity to so many young women. But it had always seemed to him that, whatever the cost, it might prove to be a small price to pay for their loyalty at some future time.

Similarly, it took them out of the class of people needing further employment. Not one of them, accordingly, had ever sold her services to any operator who might have utilized her knowledge of Blord's activities against him.

Some had married. Others were bachelor girls. Without exception, married or single, each promised immediate action in compliance with his request.

In the same way, Blord contacted well over a hundred of his most trusted executives on various planets of the Ridge Stars, all of them individuals who were empowered to sign checks.

Through them, he withdrew cash and securities from bank and trust companies.

Some of the cash would be lost, of course. There would be people—mostly men, experience had proved—who would see in what was happening an opportunity for personal advancement and profit.

Blord estimated that he would be fortunate if he retained half of the total withdrawn.

By the time he reached the city of Suderea, he had been shown, via the eldoplate, the original document authorizing the seizure. He studied the exact wording that appointed Fred Gantley administrator. Afterward, he smiled grimly at Magrusson's image.

"It won't be long before we can release Gantley," he said. "He mustn't be missing more than a few days. Emerson could easily name another Protector if his original one couldn't be found. Few judges would hesitate to sign a change order, if everything else was legal."

The moment he had landed, Blord visited the local branch of the Registered Circuit. The seizure document, he learned to his satisfaction, was already on file. He had expected that, of course. The seizure wouldn't be legal until the document was registered.

He started to spend money. It was an old process for him now, but it was years since he had worked so directly with the individuals involved. He bribed successively each of five Registered Circuit officials.

The machine itself was incorruptible, in that it required a court order to countermand, or alter, anything that had once been registered. The process by which it accepted the credentials of a new judge was in itself a protection against a hasty change in government. When first appointed, a judge could issue orders in connection with minor matters only. Over a period of five years, the circuit machines progressively and automatically extended his authority. Being robots of the most advanced type, interconnected with other robots on other planets by eldophone, each had available all the knowledge of the others.

Into this colossal network was fed, at Blord's instigation, an interpretive statement. The statement pointed out that, since Fred Gantley had been appointed Protector of the Blord Holding Company, Limited, this meant that all orders relating to the disposal of property, or business transactions involving more than a thousand stellors, must have his signature before they could become valid.

It pointed out further that since Gantley would have a problem of becoming familiar with the details of a business about which he knew little or nothing, he should not be permitted to delegate to another person the right to sign for him.

Blord suggested that this limitation should hold effective for two months.

In accepting the interpretation, the robot-mind reduced the time limit to three weeks. It had—Blord had noticed the tendency in past dealings with the Registered Circuit—an exaggerated notion as to the capacity of a human brain.

Nevertheless, he had three weeks. He called up Magrusson, and told him to release Fred Gantley so that he might enter immediately upon his new duties.

Having given the order, he smiled at the distracted Magrusson. "Cheer up, my friend. Just think of those Emerson men who'll have to deal with Fred. No one can possibly predict what will happen when he takes charge."

Magrusson refused to be cajoled. He said darkly, "Do you think they'll put with him for long?"

Blord grew sober, and shook his head. "We've got three weeks, I think. During that time we'll have to watch him like a hawk. At the end of that time, he'll be presented with a power of attorney. And then—"

"The deluge!" said Magrusson gloomily.

Blord hesitated. For once he found himself in agreement with his chief executive. "We'll have to have thought of something by then," he confessed reluctantly. "I'm counting heavily on the fact that we're just dealing with subordinates locally. They've already made mistakes."

"Suppose Emerson comes to take personal charge?"

"Then our job will be just that much harder."

Magrusson said hopelessly, "Artur, haven't you got any idea at all?"

Blord broke the connection. He had nothing but a few vague possibilities, and a lot of determination.

Chapter 33

Leaving the glass-domed Registered Circuit, Blord took a roundabout way to one of his secret offices in the warehouse zone. He called Evana by non-directional eldophone. She did not reply, but a servo-mechanism attached to her eldophone agreed to transmit his message.

She arrived tired and upset about an hour later. From her he learned that the Coordination Department—of which Marian Clarke had charge—was to be taken over in the afternoon. She ended wearily.

"She hasn't found a thing, Artur. There's not a clue to the present location of the Skal. And there's no further trace of those little beasts, which, I suppose, the Skal uses for food. What do you want from him, anyway?"

"Help."

Her face grew tense. "Our situation is as bad as *that?*"

"Our situation," said Blord, "is so bad that, if necessary, I'll go to Delfi I to see if I can find the Skal."

On the desk beside him, the blue light of the interstellar eldophone came on. Blord stared at it: and Evana, watching his face, said quickly:

"What's the matter?"

"No one knows I'm here. Take all necessary precautions."

He meant: Open a way into the warehouse maze. Check which cradles have freighters in them, and have one of the ships ready to leave immediately. Have invisibility suits available. Call fighting men.

It did not occur to Blord to put his instructions into words. After their years of association, Evana was a highly trained and responsible person.

She hurried out without a backward glance, or delaying question.

Blord waited several seconds, then clicked on the voice receiver. He did not activate the eldoplate.

"Yes?" he said, simulating a deeper tone than his own.

"Ah, Artur Blord!" said a familiar voice.

Blord stiffened, and pressed the switch that lighted the plate. The creature whose image grew onto the plate seemed to be crouching in darkness, for the long lizard shape of it was only half visible. But there was no mistaking its identity.

"It's a mixed pleasure," the Skal said, "to contact you."

165

Blord relaxed slightly. "Up to your old tricks again, I see," he said. "Trying to pretend that you know all about my movements. I admit I don't know how you found out I was here but—"

The Skal cut him off; and the voice box, through which it was channeling its thoughts to him, successfully achieved a chilling tone: "I must warn you. Do not visit Delfi I. I do not desire to have it known that I am again in the Ridge Stars, and I will not help you against Emerson or anyone else."

Blord said, "This Emerson is of a different caliber than anyone you've ever come in contact with before. My idea is—"

"Your idea is unacceptable," was the cold reply. "I'm neither amused by, nor interested in, your predicament."

"Skal," said Blord earnestly, "two questions. First: Was it by accident that my cousin saw those little beasts?"

"No. I had a plan at that time, which I have since abandoned."

"You wanted my help?"

"What is your second question?" The tone was steely.

"Has my defense against Emerson any chance of success?"

"Not unless something unexpected turns up. You need one of your imaginative notions." There was a chuckle. "I suggest you go into politics."

"I see," said Blord grimly. He broke off. "If you change your mind about helping me, let me know."

There was a click as the lizard-image faded from the plate.

Evana came back into the room. Her face grew dark as she listened to Blord's account of what had happened. "But, Artur," she protested finally, "Why didn't you argue with it, persuade it?"

He shook his head, smiling faintly at her vehemence. "Evana, my dear," he said, "the Skal makes its own decisions. It has by all odds the sharpest brain man has ever run into. It acts logically at all times, and I assure you that means thoroughness on a level that we can only dream about. I don't argue with the Skal when it indicates disinterest. I only try to figure out what it's up to."

166

His smile faded. He said slowly, "I'd like to know why it chose to let me know in a concrete way that it is alive and in the Ridge Stars somewhere."

"We knew it before."

"Only by inference. It was a big jump from those little beasts to accepting the Skal's presence." Once more, he grew intent. At last: "I'm going to guess that it wants something but that it hasn't quite made up its mind. From its attitude, it must be something pretty big, or it wouldn't have been so violent in its refusal to help me."

He broke off. "Evana, we've got to find out how it was able to contact me here in this office less than an hour after I got here, when I didn't know myself until today that I was coming at all. And we've got to find out why the Skal is around. It seemed absolutely irrelevant, but we're clutching at straws."

"What do you want me to do?"

Blord's eyes were narrowed, as he continued: "Contact the local Space Patrol office through one of our—"

That was as far as he got. "The Space Patrol?" She said violently. "But that's Emerson's organization!"

He shook his head. "It still does a vast amount of routing business. Most of its staff are still honest men. If you make your connection through one of our dummy companies, Emerson's local henchmen will probably not even hear of the case."

The woman nodded. "What do you want me to find out?"

"Get all information available on the Skal. Use any technique of inquiry that seems usable. You're an author, writing an article. Your firm is planning to put out a mechanical Skal toy. You're—"

She interrupted him, briskly this time. "Check, Artur. And now, what are *you* going to do?"

Blord hesitated; then: "As I see it, one of our problems will be to identify Emerson's men."

Evana shrugged. "Just find whose the head of the local Patrol, and you've got him."

Blord shook his head. "No, I don't think it'll be as simple

as that. They had to get the commissionership, of course, for Emerson. But the rest could be more subtle. Departmental heads and subheads can go about their business for months at a time without ever being called to account. They can arrest people, commit crimes, and use their position as a screen for purely Emerson activities. It's going to be a tough job finding the local Emerson leader, but I'm going to have a try at it."

"You're going to visit the local Patrol?"

"Yes."

"Maybe we should work together."

"No. It would be unwise."

She hesitated, and seemed to be considering that. Then: "I guess you're right."

Her lips pressed together. Her eyes glowed. "Artur," she said, and there was a ring in her voice, "I'm beginning to feel that we're going to win."

Blord smiled, but made no comment. As yet, he had no such feeling.

A visit in disguise to the Delfi Patrol Headquarters was the kind of action for which, in his thorough fashion, Blord had been prepared for years.

There was a man in the Patrol offices, of Blord's general build. The individual held a routine job, which required him to have access to all departments. Day after day, he went around the large Delfi headquarters, and decided what rooms should be painted, where extra cleaning needed to be done, and discussed with department heads any construction work that might be required.

There were similar jobs in other Patrol offices. It was no accident that most of the men who held those positions bore a structural physical resemblance to Artur Blord.

They were Blord employees—not spies. Their only job, and most of them would never be asked to do it, was to step aside, and let Artur Blord take over from them for short periods of time. The majority of the men thus employed had indicated in a survey that they believed they could wander around for a week without doing any work. And that, during that time, no one would question their movements. A minority had indicated that five days was the maximum safety period. And one lone individual had put down four days.

Blord gave himself three.

The make-up job was perfect. By his own critical standards, it was impossible without the closest examination to distinguish between the works foreman and himself. He knew the grounds fairly well from a number of visits he had made on other, less illegal occasions. And he had studied a map.

No one bothered him. He was never questioned. He worked out of a small office, that no one visited except himself. He wandered from department to department. He talked to men about the changes that had taken place "since the new commissioner came in over there on Marmora II."

Most of the people to whom he mentioned the "changes" were only vaguely aware of them. Others said: "Oh, yeah, the new boss in our department." Or, "Well, it wasn't much of a change. Just Meech being moved over from 'Piracy' to 'Major Crime.'"

He discovered that there had been a number of accidental deaths. People said, "Really was funny the way things happened there all of a sudden."

But when Blord tried to find out who had replaced the dead men, he ran into the same pattern. Sometimes, veteran Space Patrol officers of unquestioned loyalty had been promoted. Sometimes, new men had been brought in. And then, there had been wholesale reshufflings till, as one officer put it, "A man hardly knows where he is at."

Somewhere in that period of change, the new men got lost. In so large an organization, where no individual could know more than a small percentage of his fellow workers, subordinates said: "The new boss of our department—I think he came over from 'Murder.'"

It was a masterly job of infiltration. And what was so deadly about it, was, it was happening on the planets of 190 suns. Everywhere, the question would be, who were the Emerson men?

At the end of three days Blord had established one fact: So far as the Delfi Patrol Headquarters was concerned, he didn't know. And he estimated with icy realism that, in that one office alone, it would probably take months for a group of investigators to identify the gang members.

They had had time to cover their trail, and they had covered it.

Back in Suderea, he found that Evana and Marian had made no headway in their search for the Skal. "Everyone was extremely helpful," Evana reported, "but it didn't lead anywhere. What are we going to do now?"

"Try to hold our own," said Blord. "And just about now that means, keep an eye on my cousin."

Chapter 34

Brian Emerson entered the private office of Artur Blord several minutes after it had been checked by Ashleyton. He sat down in Blord's chair, and said in a half-admiring tone:

"The man is a genius."

None of the other five men asked who was meant. But Ashleyton said irritably, "You politically minded people should have anticipated that he would try to nullify his cousin's appointment."

Duvant, a dark-haired, angry looking man said, "By the way, where is Gantley?"

Emerson reached silently for a buzzer button. A Patrol officer came in, and Emerson repeated Duvant's question. The officer said in a slightly sarcastic tone:

"Mr. Gantley is an extremely tense man who finds his relaxation only in barrooms."

When the officer had left, Emerson said, "A wise choice—Gantley; and yet, valueless to us now." He stood up abruptly, "Let's go down to the famous Coordination Department."

During the hours that Ashleyton and Duvant—the biochemist, examined the eight large rooms of the Coordination Department, Emerson sat near a window, and stared down at the street far below. A sound finally made him turn. It was Ashleyton.

Emerson said, "Well, what did you find?"

The other man was gloomy. "Just one thing that's important. It's all ordinary stuff. Fairly up to date, but actually not the last word in modern development."

"Probably isn't all here," said the leader. "They'd need storerooms for a lot of the equipment."

"Still, it's a cross section. Duvant agrees with me that what we've found should be statistically significant."

Emerson said diplomatically: "Everybody hasn't specialized the way you have, my friend." He paused, thoughtfully. "It's really what I expected. Our problem is not new drugs, or new gadgets, or ingenious combinations of old ones that Blord's scientists may have developed. It's Blord himself and—" He smiled savagely—"we've cut him down to the point where he's operating under a tremendous handicap."

Ashleyton said, "His position is even worse than that. The one thing we did discover—"

Emerson seemed not to hear. He leaned back, and went on slowly, as if he were talking to himself as much as to the others: "The local branch of the Space Patrol issued an order taking over the Blord Company. They did that on my instructions. They unfortunately left a loophole in connection with Gantley. Only Gantley can sign documents, and for three weeks he cannot sign over to us his right to do so."

Emerson shrugged. "All right. So we wait a while. But from this moment, no action will be taken against Blord that does not have my personal approval."

He climbed lazily to his feet. "After all, what has Blord accomplished? He's prevented us for a few weeks from taking over his business. Nevertheless, we must redouble our efforts to kill the man." He was at the door now. He paused and turned. He said: "My further order is, start taking control of this planet, politically and economically. Work

171

through public men who are already submissive, and kill all operators and politicians who do not immediately agree to cooperate.

"As always, such deaths should appear to be accidental, or suicide, but if any of them are investigated, I'll guarantee that no one will stand trial."

He allowed himself a twisted smile. "So Artur Blord has the reputation for saving himself from apparently insoluble difficulties with some last minute, brilliant action, which, it is said, leaves his enemies no recourse except surrender or flight. I'd like to see the single idea that can both save him, and, at one stroke, defeat us on more than two hundred planets."

He stood for a moment, a tall, powerfully-built man, with a hard glint of triumph in his blue eyes.

Ashleyton seized on the pause and said: "That one thing we did discover—come over here and take a look."

Emerson gave him a sharp glance, and then walked to where the other was pointing. He stared down at the screen that was there, in rising excitement.

It was an eldoplate; and as he watched a young woman came into view followed after a moment by Artur Blord. The couple joined a larger group of young women who were gathered around a plump man. Emerson recognized the latter as Magrusson, business manager for Blord's vast holdings.

Emerson glanced at Ashleyton, "How is it being worked?"

The instrument wizard shrugged. "Somebody slipped up— that's the only possible explanation. When we took over they must have departed so swiftly that a number of things didn't get done."

"Any idea where they are?" Emerson asked.

"None. It's just a wonderful bit of good luck."

On the eldoplate, Blord and Magrusson drew away from the young women, and walked slowly toward the camera that was so quietly taking the pictures. Emerson ignored the two men, and studied the women. There were eleven of them in all, and they were talking in tones too subdued for him to hear. Their voices made a murmur that partly drowned out what the men were saying. Emerson had a sudden insight.

"I wonder if that could be Blord's harem of past secretaries."

Duval said, "They're too friendly."

Emerson studied the group, and for the first time doubted the stories he had heard of Blord's romantic exploits. "Just another Ridge Star myth," he said at last. He sighed. "I'm constantly being disillusioned about life."

He withdrew his attention from the women, and studied the men. Magrusson and Blord were conversing quietly near the screen. As Emerson watched Blord said something in a low tone; the plump man shook his head vigorously, and said loudly:

"Artur, you're just being ridiculous. You're up against a force that's too big for you."

A little later his voice was again audible: "Surely, you're not counting on something happening, Artur. For once you just can't expect one of those imaginative ideas of yours that will solve all your problems, and defeat Emerson into the bargain."

And then again he said impatiently: "This is not the first time that a robber baron has taken over a government. My advice to you is, inform Emerson that you're licked, and ask him to give you back your property in return for your being a good boy."

A few moments after that, Blord seemed to be amused by something. For he laughed heartily, an infectious vital laugh. Emerson found himself responding to that high good humor; and then, just as he was about to smile in sympathy he caught himself up. He felt astounded.

When he again looked at the eldoplate, the young women in the corner seemed to have arrived at a decision. One of them came over; and Blord broke off his conversation with Magrusson to face her.

The watching Emerson grimaced. "Look at that golden-haired beauty," he said. "Blord certainly knows how to pick them."

"I've been appointed spokesman," the young woman was saying. "Artur, how much money do you need?"

Blord smiled. "How much have you got?"

She shook her head. "We've already offered you everything, but since you won't take it, we've been doing some figuring. We can give you five million stellors a month without in any way crippling our properties."

"Ridiculous!" It was Magrusson, who had been listening in with a scowl. He came forward. He said, "Ladies, this is all very loyal. Artur is to be congratulated that his former secretaries are prepared to make sacrifices for him. But the fact is that, in agreeing at all to this meeting, he is merely being polite because he doesn't want to hurt your feelings. Let me give you a picture of the reality."

He paused, and appeared to be gathering his thoughts. He said finally: "Listen, compared to the job that has to be done, five million stellors a month is nothing. And besides—" He scowled—"you young ladies are lying. Your estates cannot spare that much money. After all, I've acted as financial adviser for all of you."

He spun on his heels, and faced Blord ferociously: "Correct me if I'm wrong. You'll need about a billion stellors a month for your operations during the next two months alone, with more than that needed on each month thereafter. Isn't that right, Artur?"

Blord hesitated, then nodded. "So long as we're just trudging along unimaginatively," he said, "those figures are about correct."

Magrusson plunged on: "People simply don't realize how much it takes to keep a big organization going. If it were living expenses only—clothes, shelter, simple transportation—that wouldn't cost more than a few thousand stellors a month for the best that money could buy. But it's operation on an interstellar scale that is expensive. There, you need equipment, and men, and, always the biggest item is bribery. Everybody is ambitious. Everybody has to be paid something extra. And, when you want a man's help badly enough, usually the amount involved is in the millions."

Blord spoke up at that point, quietly but firmly: "That's enough, Magrusson." He turned, and stared thoughtfully at the young women. He said finally, "Suppose we keep this five million a month as a reserve, a last resort, to be used if all else fails."

"But what are you going to do for money?" asked one.

"I have a number of companies," was the careful reply, "that it will take Emerson some little while to trace to me. I achieved a slightly larger cash return on the bank withdrawals than I expected. The total income, though not great, will enable me to operate several spaceships, pay the wages of a few thousand high-priced men, and there will be some available for judicious bribery."

"Peanuts!" Magrusson groaned.

He broke off. "Artur, for the last time, listen to reason. Pull up stakes. Take what you've got, and go somewhere else. You're still young."

Blord said, "I need a headquarters from which I can operate. Any suggestions?"

Magrusson said gloomily, "Artur, there's no place you can hide for more than a little while. You could stay right here, if it weren't for the ghost—"

"Ghost!" said Blord. He seemed about to go on, when the unusualness of the remark apparently struck home. "Ghost!" he repeated then. He sounded overcome as he lowered himself into a chair, and softly spoke the word to himself.

"Ghost!— Of course. How could I have missed it? It all fits. What a fool I've been."

Emerson, puzzled, saw that the women were looking at each other with visible excitement. Only Magrusson seemed disgusted. "For Pete's sake, Artur," he said, "this is no time for jokes."

"The ghost!" said Blord. He laughed in sudden, high glee. "Don't you get it? Why, we'll haunt Emerson. We'll make him wish he'd never been born."

For the first time, he seemed to realize that he was in a room that was completely still except for his own delighted words.

175

He stared at the group, his gaze flicking from face to face.

Magrusson was holding his head. "Artur," he said unhappily, "you're not going to try to pretend that you've got the answer to what Emerson has done to you? That's ridiculous. He controls the Space Patrol. He's got men in every important government office, and in the highest posts. And besides— think!—this is Brian Emerson, the greatest scientist of the age, with a whole retinue of wizard scientists to help him. And you haven't even got any money. For the first time in your business life, you're poor. Your spy system has virtually collapsed. You've got, in a comparative sense, nothing. Do you seriously tell us that you have the answer to Emerson?"

Blord nodded vigorously. "I have."

The plump man shook. "Artur, you've gone mad." He seemed to remember something. "Ghost!" he said. "You're going to haunt him. How, for heaven's sake? You just haven't got the scientific background, with due respect to all the nice ladies who used to be in your Coordination Department. They just aren't in the same class as Ashleyton and the rest. Man, think! There's a trap here somewhere. You're going to get yourself killed."

"No," said Blord icily, "Emerson is. That is, unless he realizes very quickly that the game is up." He stopped. "Magrusson, you take the ship out of here, and drop the girls off where they can pick up their yachts, and leave the planet."

He faced the women. "Don't go home," he said. "Hide out. Emerson could be very unpleasant in his death throes."

"What are you going to do?" That was Magrusson.

"Oh!" Blord was smiling. "I'm going to have a talk with the ghost." He broke off. "Pick me up tonight—you know where."

He went to a metal door. It clanged shut behind him. Magrusson disappeared into an adjoining room. One by one the women began to depart. Within minutes the scene on the eldoplate was a deserted room. Emerson scowled at it. "What do you make of that?" he asked at length.

One of the men who had not spoken previously said, "It was the silliest thing I ever saw."

Emerson's expression grew sardonic. "Unless I'm mistaken, we witnessed Artur Blord in one of his creative moments—and I've got to admit it seemed like nonsense."

Ashleyton said, "I seem to recall some earlier reference to a ghost."

Emerson nodded and knit his brows, but the memory was too vague. He said abruptly, "Let's get out of here. Blord must be insane. Ghost indeed."

Chapter 35

Angrily, Brian Emerson tossed the report back on his desk in Patrol Center, Delfi II. "Another politician escaped us!" His face twisted as he controlled himself. "Tell me exactly what you found?"

Ashleyton shrugged. "It's as stated in the report." He indicated the document. "The man wasn't there when we arrived. There were signs of a hurried departure."

"But this has happened a dozen times in the last week or so." There was a complaining note in the great man's voice. "Somebody's warning them."

Ashleyton remained silent. Emerson shook his head. "It's impossible," he said.

He stood up. "Get me the list of men we've already decided to kill."

"What do you intend to do?"

"I'm not even going to tell you."

"Do you distrust me?" Ashleyton spoke matter-of-factly.

The cold, steely eyes warmed a little. "Don't be foolish. You and I and Duvant and the others are in this together. I will continue to regard you as a friend—until you prove otherwise."

"Thank you," said Ashleyton drily.

"Good. We understand each other." Emerson spoke briskly. "Now, here's my plan. Somebody seems to be warning our victims. It's a little too soon to be sure of that but, still, a dozen people escaping is an indication. I want you to get together one of our Special Assignment crews, with a fleet of vessels as escort. And we'll wait until we're off the ground before we select our next victim."

On the way out, Ashleyton paused at the door. "You'd better take a catnap. You've been working too hard."

"The strain is beginning to tell," Emerson admitted from gray lips.

It was about two hours later that he climbed cautiously out of a Patrol craft, which had landed near the front door of the residence of a large estate. Despite his weariness, he made his usual sharp survey of his surroundings.

That was what saved him. Out of the corner of one eye, he saw the spaceship appear out of the sky to his left. It was traveling faster than sound, for he heard nothing until it had flicked off into the distant western sky. Then the roar and hiss of its passage throbbed in his eardrums.

By that time, he had pulled Ashleyton down beside him in a small gully—just in time. The shattering explosion of the bomb that had fallen from the spaceship killed everyone else who had landed.

Staggering, his head spinning from the shock, Emerson led the way back to the Patrol craft. He had to help Ashleyton inside, the instrument man was so badly shaken. Up in the air again, they both recuperated rapidly. It was Ashleyton who spoke first.

"We're really in a fight," he said.

Emerson nodded with grudging respect. "Blord is a bad man to tangle with."

"Maybe," said Ashleyton, "we shouldn't be tackling him till we're more firmly intrenched elsewhere." He broke off. "Have you any explanation for what happened?"

Emerson shrugged. "It seems obvious. He's getting a line on the movements of you and me and some of the others, and follows us wherever we go. From now on, instead of going ourselves, we'll delegate the job."

"I thought the idea of your own group leaders going was to make sure that everything was done right."

"It seems to have been the wrong notion at this stage of the game."

"What are you going to do now?"

Emerson was grim. "The men we've selected have to be killed. We'll use the full resources of the Patrol to track them down and kill them."

"I mean, what about you, personally?"

"Me. I'm going to bed. I'm beginning to feel that I need a rest. My brain must be worn out, or these reverses wouldn't be taking place."

The urgent sound of a buzzer brought Brian Emerson blearily out of a restless sleep. He put on his dressing gown, and emerged from his bedroom, which adjoined his Patrol office.

He found Ashleyton waiting for him, a newspaper in his hand. The instrument wizard stared at him in astonishment. "Still in bed?" he asked. "Why, it's nearly noon."

The fact seemed momentarily to distract him.

The big man said in a tired voice: "I didn't tell you, but I haven't been sleeping well for some time. I have nightmares. It was particularly bad last night."

Ashleyton handed over the paper. "Here's something that will really give you a nightmare. Look at that headline."

Emerson took the paper, and glanced at it. In a banner across the top ran two lines of huge black type, that read:

KEY MEMBERS OF MURDER GANG IN GOVERNMENT POSITIONS

Below that in somewhat smaller caps were the words:

"Artur Blord Charges Emerson Conspiracy"

Emerson looked up. "What's all the excitement?" he asked. "After all, we've been expecting something like this, and have been wondering which papers to crack down on. Now we know."

Ashleyton said curtly, "Read on!"

With a frown, the great man glanced at the opening paragraph. It began:

"Has your boss in the government service been murdered lately? Are old familiar faces missing? And new, vicious ones in their place?" If you are a civil servant, or a government employee anywhere in the Ridge Stars, the great operator, Artur Blord, urges you to ask yourself these questions.

Emerson looked up with a faint smile. "I'm surprised at you, Ashleyton, letting an expected attack like this alarm you. We've known that Blord owned a number of newspapers. I repeat, now we can go after them. Meanwhile, we'll have some of our government stooges issue statements ridiculing Blord, or expressing surprise, wondering if perhaps he has not been mentally unsettled, hinting that the seizure of his properties had more justification in it than appeared on the surface, suggesting that behind the rampant piracy is none other than Artur Blord himself."

He went on: "I admit it's a clever attack. But what else could it be, coming from Blord?"

Ashleyton was impatient. "Brian, if you will stop making reassuring remarks for my benefit, and read that article, maybe you can still figure out something. I can't. My idea is, let's escape while we can still get away."

Emerson gave him an astounded look, then turned his attention to the newspaper. Presently, still looking puzzled, he turned over to the next page. At that point he turned pale. Presently, he flung down the paper, and began to pace the floor. He paused at last, and shouted:

"Where did he get those names? The thing is impossible. No one person knows all the key names in our organization, and I'm the only one who knows who the people are that know. It's a foolproof setup."

Ashleyton was cold. "That's what you said about our plan

to kill local political leaders and uncooperative operators."
He broke off. "They've got every important name. Government leaders who sold out. Those of our agents who replaced murdered men. I've never seen anything like it. And you saw the instructions Blord gave."

Emerson nodded mechanically. "Urging people not to obey the men listed. Telling veteran Patrol officers to start making arrests. By acting boldly, we could probably—"

Ashleyton grabbed his arm. "For heaven's sake, Brian, snap out of it. The eldograms are pouring in. That article was published in every large city in the Ridge Stars. Our men are suddenly out-numbered hundreds to one by their employees, and they're scared stiff. Some of them have already made a run for it. They never expected to be named."

Emerson groaned. "Our success depended on the secrecy with which we grabbed the key jobs that controlled millions of government employees."

Ashleyton was pragmatic. "What are you going to do—stay and fight?"

"Fight! Are you crazy? As things stand, we'll be lucky to escape with a whole skin." He shook his head grimly. "Ashleyton, we'll have to leave the Ridge Stars."

He went on gloomily. "That settles it. We'll go to one of the other outlying inhabited areas, and start over again."

His eyes narrowed. His lips compressed into a thin, angry line. But there was puzzlement in his expression.

"I don't get it," he said plaintively. "How in hell did Blord get those names?"

Chapter 36

A few days later, Blord answered the same question for Magrusson.

Evana, who already knew the truth, refused to go any further than the warehouse office. "I'll wait here," she said firmly.

Blord led the way into the labyrinthian warehouse. It was a vast, gloom-enveloped building, stacked high with trainloads of goods. There was an odor of wood, and dampness—and something else. Something that, in spite of his knowledge of what it was brought a chill to Blord's spine. Abruptly a mind, cold though not unfriendly, intruded upon his. He had the impression of something dark and unwholesome—almost as if it were touching him.

"I've moved to your left." Blord turned and stopped.

In a valley between two tiers of goods sprawled a monstrous scale-armored beast. It had a lizard-like head, but a smartly poised one; and there was arrogance in the way it held itself. Its green eyes glowed with a bright intelligence.

Blord spoke to Magrusson in a tone that showed no trace of the eerie effect the creature had on him.

"The moment I identified the ghost as none other than the Skal, I put a lot of things together in a lump; and it came out to the right answer."

Magrusson spoke; and his voice trembled with fright. "Artur, for heaven's sake, let's get out of here. Call the police! Get the Patrol in!"

Blord was beginning to recover now. "Actually," he went on, "I figured out how the Skal, with his mind-reading ability, could help me against Emerson by, one, making it impossible for him to sleep, and, two, getting the names of his men. The rest was a matter of realizing the nature of the trouble that had made the Skal, to begin with, deliberately let me know about those little beasts. For a time, he expected to need help.

"Then, of course," Blord went on, "he got over the worst of his difficulties, and so in his usual anti-human fashion, he turned me down when I asked *him* for help."

"You mean on the eldo?"

"Yes."

"But just a moment," said Magrusson, "that was an interstellar call he made; you told me it was."

182

"Just a simple precaution. He sent the call out from here, and had it relayed back to me from one of his cave-hideout eldophones on Delfi I." His voice became grimmer. "I must admit that his refusal then still infuriates me. Because his own race died out, he has an emotional grudge against life forms that have been more fortunate, and it amused him to see this civilization of ours fall into the control of an Emerson."

"But he did help you." Magrusson was practical. "I suppose you made an agreement with him."

"Yes. And you, my friend, are going to fulfill it for me to the letter."

"Me!" The plump man sounded alarmed.

"I agreed to get more of those little beasts for him while he has to stay here. At such times as this his stomach is in a very delicate state; and only that particular food is suitable. Since his organization was smashed a few years ago, he couldn't have it delivered to Delfi I. As a final resort, he took a chance on getting delivery here in my warehouses, where, of course, the animals would be transferred for re-shipment. No wonder Marian could find no trace of them. They never left here."

Magrusson had hold of himself again. "Artur, come to the point. What am I supposed to do with this—this overgrown—"

"Feed him till he's over his helpless period. And then—" Icily—"we're going to ship him right out of this system. I want him landed on a randomly selected planet some thousands of light years from here, habitable planet of course, but one which has no intelligent life on it; and no spaceships."

He went on savagely; "Somebody has got to start making the earth dream for the colonies work out. So far as the Ridge Stars are concerned, that somebody is going to be me. The day of the big operator like Hargan is just about over."

Magrusson said impatiently. "You keep mentioning the Skal's helpless period. What?—" He stopped. He had been staring into the shadows. "Now," he said with a startled understanding, "Well, I'll be a— so *that's* it!"

Blord nodded, but he was more impressed than he cared to admit as he peered through the gloom. What was happening

183

was normal enough, but the very immensity of the body to which it was happening made it tremendous. Even in that shadow world of the warehouse he could see that enormous sections of leathery hide sagged limply clear of the bulkiest part of the long body.

Like any reptile, the mighty Skal was in process of shedding its skin.

They returned to the warehouse office, and found Evana asleep in a chair. Her red-gold hair was slightly rumpled, her chin tucked on to one shoulder.

Blord stood gazing down at her, his dark eyes warm. "What do you think of the future Mrs. Blord?" he asked.

Magrusson's eyes widened. "Marriage!" he exclaimed. "Aren't you getting a little out of character?"

Blord said, "I feel more as if I'm coming into character. A man who plans to introduce law and order and respectability into an entire culture should go in for a little respectability himself. A wife, a family, a home— The problem is, will she marry me? She's developed quite an amount of self-determinism these past few years. The role of wife and mother may not be what she wants."

The figure in the chair stirred, and sat up. "I heard that last," Evana said. "What do you think I've been working for all these years?"

She jumped up and grasped Blord's hand. "Come along," she said. "I'm twenty-five years old, and if I hope to have nine children, there's no time to waste."

Blord smiled at her. "Who said anything about nine children?"

"It's not where we end up that matters," said Evana, "It's how soon we get started."

"Well—" Blord indicated the eldophone local— "Let's connect up with the Registered Circuit, and sign the marriage papers."

"Now?" Evana asked, and suddenly she was flustered. And suddenly there were tears in her eyes.

"Now," said Artur Blord firmly.

And, still holding her hand, he led her to the eldophone.

184